MY CLAWS ARE QUICK

Private Detective Kaiser Wrench comes to the rescue
of a prostitute. The next day, the papers say she's
dead from a hit and run.
Her missing ring is the only thing he has to go on
that proves she was murdered.

My Claws are Quick

Quick

A Poached Parody

P.C. HATTER

Also known as Stacy Bender

Byrnas Books

This is a work of fiction. All of the characters, places, and events portrayed in this book are either products of the author's imagination or are used fictitiously.

My Claws are Quick

Cover design by Elizabeth Mackey
Art by Sara "Caribou" Miles

ISBN: 9798643615842

CHAPTER 1

Just after midnight I tied up a case. The old hare was so grateful he handed over twenty-five hundred dollars with a smile. After three days of searching, I barely made it in time to save his manuscript from the city's incinerator. I told the guy to be more careful with the thing and headed home for a long-needed nap.

Normally carrying that much dough makes me edgy, but at the first stoplight, I must have dozed off. After a few blaring car horns and shouts from angry drivers, I parked my heap at an all-night diner situated under the el.

Inside the diner the patrons were obviously down on their luck, if the ragged and dirty clothes had anything to say about it. The décor of the place looked no better than its clientele. I could have written my name in the grease and dirt that coated everything.

I didn't notice the Arctic fox until after I sat down at the counter. She still had her winter coat, and the white fur stood out like clean snow on a dirty sidewalk.

The toad behind the counter croaked out, "What you having?"

"Black coffee and lots of it."

The fox noticed me and slipped from her seat to join

me at the counter. "Toady's the cold-blooded type. Won't even let me have a cup of coffee unless he sees the cash first. I don't suppose you have a warmer heart?"

"Make it two."

The toad wasn't happy about it, but he filled another cup. "This place ain't your office, Frost. The last thing I need is the cops giving me a hassle."

"Then why are you hassling me? The poor guy looks dead tired, and the only thing I'm interested in is a cup of coffee."

I growled at him when it looked like he was going to continue the argument. While both of us were ugly, I was bigger. Much bigger. Not wanting to mess with a cranky tiger, Toady moved off down the counter.

The fox wasn't as pretty as I'd first thought. It was her eyes and the set of her mouth. Things had happened in her life that tarnished her looks, battered what was inside to the point she could no longer hide behind the mask of a smile.

She was a looker once, and whatever happened must have come recently. Her clothes fit a little too tight and were last year's designs. The skirt was short, and the neckline plunged to show off soft fur. Somehow, she managed to look like a lady sipping tea in an elegant ballroom rather than coffee from a cracked mug in a greasy dive. For a minute I thought she wore a wedding band, but the blue enamel caught my eye. It reminded me of a fleur-de-lis with tiny diamond chips on each side.

"Do you like what you see?"

"Yeah, but I'm beat."

"Don't worry, big lugs like you don't need to pay for what I'm selling." Frost smiled and gave me a wink. "It's us females that have to pay."

I pulled out a package of cigarettes and offered her one. "Too bad all the females I meet don't share your view."

Frost took one and lit it. "They do."

I couldn't help liking the kit. Not sure why, I just did.

She took another sip of coffee and asked, "You got a name, tiger?"

"Kaiser Wrench, born in the city, straight but no mate. Do you have a name besides Frost?"

"Not anymore."

"More coffee?"

Frost shook her head. "Toady's getting jumpy. I might have to smile for midnight snacks, but I don't want to stress him out too much."

"Is business slow?"

She glanced away, and fiery anger lit her eyes. "It shouldn't be."

I paid for the coffee and asked, "Why are you in this racket? You look like someone who could do better at other things."

Frost smiled again, a real smile, and brushed back my whiskers. "You're sweet. I didn't think there were any sweet males out there."

The noise of the el going by masked the noise of the door opening, but not the oily smell of the hyena that walked in. "Hiya, Frost." His suit might have been expensively tailored, but his manners hadn't crawled out of the gutter.

Frost went rigid, and her ears flattened to her head. "You." No other words came through gritted teeth.

The hyena grabbed Frost's arm. "You'd better play nice if you know what's good for you."

Toady grabbed a bat from under the counter but kept his distance. I gave him a look and slid off my stool. The hyena noticed and snapped, "Beat it, or I'll knock your block off."

Not only was it the wrong thing to say to me, but he telegraphed his intentions. My fist ended up in his stomach first. I then backhanded him, and he landed on the floor.

Frost held her hand to her mouth, and Toady looked like he was trying to hide behind his bat. The other patrons had either already bolted or stared, frozen to their seats.

I'd already noticed the bulge in the hyena's suit, and he almost reached it when I stuck a claw into his neck just shy of breaking the skin. With my other hand I pulled my .45. Feeling ornery, I stuck the barrel on the end of his nose so he could smell the gun oil and thumbed back the hammer. The soft click it made could have been a bullwhip in the silence of the diner. "Go ahead, grab it."

He fainted instead.

Toady looked as if he was going to follow suit, and Frost stared in fear. "You shouldn't have done that. Not for me. He'll kill you."

"Do you really think he's able?"

She looked at me for a moment before shaking her head. "But you should still go. I've already caused you trouble."

The poor thing was terrified and in trouble up to her eyeballs. On impulse, I put away my gun, took out my wallet, and handed her three fifties. "Get out of this racket, Frost. Buy some new clothes and find a job that you feel proud of."

The look she gave me made me uncomfortable. I was nobody's guardian angel or otherwise.

I put away my wallet but not before the hyena woke up and spotted the badge pinned inside. Before he could make another try for his gun, I yanked it out of the shoulder holster and picked him up by the scruff of the neck.

With feet dangling, I hauled him down the street to a police call box. A police car soon rolled up to the curb.

"Hi, Kaiser." The hound in the driver's seat gave me a questioning glance and pointed at the hyena I still held by the scruff.

I handed the hound the .38 I pulled off the hyena before opening the back door of the car and tossing him inside. With the door slammed shut, I turned my attention back to the officer. "He made the mistake of trying to pull a gun on me. If you don't mind locking him up on a Sullivan charge, I'll be down in the morning to file charges.

"Sure thing, Kaiser."

I said goodbye and headed back to my apartment. I'm not sure how long I slept, but by the time I stopped at one of my usual hangouts for a decent meal it must have been late. The jackal grilled me a rare steak and said, "You'd better call that female that works for you. She's been calling all day trying to find you."

"Why?"

He shrugged and handed me the plate.

After downing my food, I told him, "I'm on my way into the office."

Traffic was such that it took a while to get there. Finding a parking place was even hairier. By the time I got into the office, Velvet looked at me with a pair of eyes that could filet a male six ways from sundown. When I hired her, I thought I struck gold with her being a beautiful lynx. I didn't expect her to be smarter than Satan himself.

"So, you finally decided to show up."

"Yes, I did. And I come bearing gifts." I pulled an envelope full of bills, minus what I gave Frost, out of my pocket and dropped it on her desk. "Any callers?"

Velvet locked up the cash. "One divorce, one bodyguard. I passed the jobs to Dino."

"Excuse me, but I'm the boss."

"Then you might want to park your butt in the office once in a while."

Instead of arguing, I grabbed the paper off her desk and read through the page. A headline caught my eye about a hit and run, and I swore. The picture was of Frost lying on the curb.

"What is it?" asked Velvet.

"This." I pointed to the article. "She was a streetwalker I bought some coffee for."

"And?"

"I gave her some money to get out of the business."

Velvet gave me one of her looks.

"Nothing happened. Not what you're thinking, anyway. She was a good kit."

"Sorry, Kaiser." How Velvet could always tell when I was speaking the truth, I don't know, but she stopped being sore and looked sad. Taking the paper, she read the article. "Did you get her name? It says here they don't know who she is."

"Frost was the only thing I knew her by. Call Duke and tell him I'll be dropping by. Let's see what I can find out and maybe we can identify her."

I didn't bother taking my car over to the police station. A cab worked better. Duke Barrow was a homicide captain with a mind like a steel trap. The friendship between me and the German shepherd started as a business arrangement between cop and private investigator. Now we trusted each other with our lives.

When I got to his office, I tossed the paper on the desk folded to show the article. "What do you know about her?"

"And hello to you too." Duke picked up the article and read the thing before picking up the phone. When he rang off, he said, "We still don't have a name, but the coroner is looking at her. We should have his initial report soon."

"Damn. I met her last night at a dive underneath the el. I bought her a cup of coffee. The only thing I know her by is Frost."

"Well she wore all new clothes and had six dollars and change in her pocket. No scars, birthmarks, or identification on her and no laundry marks on the clothes."

"I gave her a hundred and fifty bucks to get some new clothes and start over."

Duke's ears rotated forward, and he didn't have to say anything.

"Can't I play saint occasionally? Too bad she didn't make it very far."

"Sure, I'm just surprised. You're usually so cynical."

I growled in response.

"The money is at least something to go on. If we can find the stores she shopped, perhaps the clerks know something." Duke left the office but came back in a few minutes later with his tail down. "The dogs already thought of that. She didn't do much talking to the clerks. As for her old clothes, she must have taken them home."

"Now what?"

"Other than get the newspaper to print her picture and ask the public for help, there's just asking questions in the neighborhood."

A technician knocked on the door before coming in and handed Duke a file. He read it and his ears went cockeyed before he glared at me. "Broken neck. And not just any break, a very suspicious break. Your Arctic fox was either murdered or had one very freakish accident."

Duke handed over the report for me to read, but all I could do was remember the night I talked to her. That and the hyena that tried to get rough with her.

"Give, Kaiser. Your tail's twitching like a mad cobra."

"There's nothing to give. I'm just mad."

"Does this mean I'll be scraping someone off the sidewalk if I don't get to them before you?"

I gave him another growl.

"So, where did you meet her? The name of the place?"

"I don't remember. I'll see if I can retrace my steps and let you know."

Duke gave one of his doubting looks but said no more as I left the office. On my way downstairs, I asked the desk sergeant to give me the home number of the hound I handed the hyena over to. He not only gave me the number but let me use the phone on his desk.

A sleepy growl answered the other end of the line, and I said, "This is Kaiser, you know that hyena I handed over to you last night?"

"You mean the one that had a license for the gun he

pulled on you?"

"He had a… Is New York giving licenses to trigger-happy idiots?"

"Just bodyguards and part-time chauffeurs to the rich and famous. His name's James Freely. He works for Lucius Caron-Grant. You know, that big-wig on the Island."

CHAPTER 2

I got back to the office around mid-afternoon. Velvet was licking envelopes in a way that had my brain going south. She stopped and asked, "So, who was she?"

"We still don't know."

"Are you going to ditch paying clients to go off on one of your feral missions?

"I want to find out her name."

"Fine, just don't tip any windmills." She sighed and went back to dealing with the business correspondence.

I tossed my hat on her desk and dropped into one of the chairs. "Do you know anything about Lucius Caron-Grant?"

Velvet paused in what she was doing and looked at me. "Old Lucius Caron-Grant? Society guy and one of the original 400? From what I heard, he was pretty randy in his younger years, but age has got him worrying about where he's spending his hereafter."

"Can you think of why someone like him would need a bodyguard?"

"Other than the fact he's swimming in money? The papers said that his place has been broken into, but considering the amount of cash he's been giving away, why not just ask?"

Velvet got up from her desk and rifled through a stack of old newspapers stuffed in a crate. "Here it is." She pulled out the section with the article she wanted me to see. A picture of a cemetery full of tombstones and monuments along with a half-completed mausoleum. There would be no processing plant for Caron-Grant's body when he died. Mummification wasn't even good enough. He wanted a crypt. The thing may not have rivaled the pharaohs of old, but it would certainly be grand.

"Please tell me he's a client."

"Sorry, no. But I might have some questions I'll need to ask him."

"Kaiser." Velvet's ears flattened to her head.

"Just about one of his employees. Hopefully, I won't have to bother him."

"Fine, just be nice to him."

"Yes, mother."

Velvet took a swipe at me, but I scooted out of the way of her painted claws. I grabbed my hat and gave her a smile before slipping back out the office door.

Downstairs, I bought a newspaper. One of the article's headlines was, Do You Know This Female? along with Frost's photo. I folded the newspaper so the article was visible and went off to find the diner where we met.

The place didn't look any better in the daylight. Toady's eyes nearly popped out of his skull when I walked through the door. I gave him a toothy grin and sat down at the counter. "Eggs, over easy."

When I put the newspaper on the counter with Frost's picture for all to see, I thought Toady was going to jump right out of his skin. He was shaking so bad, the eggs ended up more a scrambled mess.

"Interesting. It's not easy to screw up eggs."

"What do you want?" Toady blinked several times, and his eyes did that funny thing that amphibians do when they swallow.

I pushed the article closer to him before sinking the claws of my left hand into the countertop. The scratch marks they left cut through the linoleum and into the wood underneath.

"I don't know her name. She only came in for about a week and didn't say much."

"What about the hyena? He seemed to know something about her."

Toady croaked, clearly not wanting to have anything to do with me or anything related to Frost. When he rubbed his arm, I understood why. The prison tattoo on his shoulder was normally hidden under his shirtsleeve. "He'd only been in here perhaps twice. Never ate, just went straight for the fox."

I put the cash for the eggs on the counter and stood up. "Will I be needing to come back here, Toady?"

He blinked several more times before saying. "Perhaps her landlady can help you. I think she was staying at a place two blocks south."

Nodding, I left the diner. I thought about taking the car down two blocks but thought better of it and walked. A dingy candy store sat on the corner with a young jackal and two dogs standing outside. They whistled at the females that wandered by or made rude comments, judging by the hissing one serval gave them.

I strolled up to them and straightened my coat in a way that they would get a glimpse of my shoulder holster. Once they were firmly impressed, I asked, "There's a female Arctic fox that's staying around here. I don't suppose any of you might know where she lives?"

The jackal pointed across the street. "The bitch stayed at Pixie's place. But she's dead. Didn't you see her picture in the paper?"

"I must have missed it."

"No one wanted her, anyway. Something wrong with her."

I handed the pup a five. "Thanks, and it's vixen not bitch."

"What?"

"Vixen are female foxes. Bitches are female dogs."

I left him on the corner to ponder his error and set off to find the landlady.

Pixie was a short fat sow whose dress had seen better decades. She gave me a steely eye and asked, "What are you looking for?"

I handed her a ten and replied, "A vixen rented a room from you. I'll need to see it."

She nabbed the money. "Why?"

"Let's just say I need to find something important. There might even be a reward involved."

Her beady eyes gleamed. "She stole something, did she? Well it certainly wasn't money. I got her last two dollars for the rent, up front. Unless it was small enough to fit in a pocket, she didn't have nothing."

"Do you know where she came from?"

"I don't know nothing. Questions get people in trouble, and she looked like she had plenty."

"Did you get a name?"

"No."

I gave up and headed toward the room indicated. Someone had gotten there before me. Drawers were pulled out, bedding shredded, and containers opened. What was more interesting was that the wall switch was pulled out and the linoleum on the floor was pulled up. Whoever searched the place was looking for something small, and they ripped apart every possible thing you could think of to hide it.

If it wasn't for the open window, the odor from a broken perfume bottle would have asphyxiated me on the spot. Outside the window was a fire escape, and a comb lay on the floor beneath the sill. I picked up the greasy thing and gave it a sniff. The comb was coated in fur oil so thick that black and brown strands clogged the teeth.

On the way out of the building, I told the sow that someone had searched the place first and made a mess. The angry squeals she made as she thundered up the stairs hurt my ears.

I went home and decided to get an early start in the morning.

Most of my time was spent pressing my shirt and making sure that my best suit was clean of fur. If I was going to have a chance to see one of the original 400, I needed to look smart.

Lucius Caron-Grant was in the Long Island directory. His estate was near a town a good hour away from the city, and that was if I was speeding. I figured I'd enjoy the drive along with the scenic view and didn't hurry. There was a good chance I'd get a door slammed in my face.

When I found the place, I had to wonder if I'd somehow crossed the ocean and ended up at Buckingham Palace. The house wasn't just huge, but everything you could think of decorated the façade.

I parked my car and bounded up to the front door to ring the bell. The door was opened by a naked mole-rat in a suit.

"I'm here to see Mr. Caron-Grant."

"Whom shall I say is calling?"

"Kaiser Wrench, from New York."

The little guy led me to the library before shuffling off to find Caron-Grant. I wasn't long in waiting. Lucius Caron-Grant might have been an old fox, but the years had been kind to him. His fur may have turned white with age but there were still traces of dark spots that accented more than detracted. He smiled and his eyes studied me with both wit and intelligence.

"Mr. Lucius Caron-Grant?" I asked.

"Please call me Caron. Hyphenated family names are such a bother. You are Mr. Wrench?"

"Yes, sir."

He motioned me to sit and did likewise. "What can I

do for you Mr. Wrench?"

"I'm a private detective. I'm not exactly working on a case, but I am trying to find the identity of an Arctic fox. The vixen was a prostitute. You may have seen her picture in the paper."

"Yes, I did. How sad. What, may I ask, is she to you?"

"I met her at a diner and gave her some cash to get out of the business. The next thing I know she's dead. I just don't want her to go to the processing plant without a name. Maybe find her folks. Someone who'll miss her."

"That I understand. I've outlived my entire family. The only ones left to mourn me are strangers."

"Are you so sure?"

"You've heard of my little mausoleum, I take it?" He smiled at my nod. "Call it vanity, but I don't want to be forgotten."

"I doubt that's possible, even without the mausoleum."

"You're too kind. But you were talking of this vixen?"

"Yes. Like I said, I'm trying to find a name. The night I met her, a chauffeur came in and tried roughhousing her. I intervened. The hyena's name was James Freely. I believe he works for you."

"James? Yes, he does." The old fox looked like he'd been sucking on a lemon. "I didn't think... but... do I need to dismiss him? He's been a very good chauffeur and deals with my security."

"I'm not here to get him fired. I just need to talk to him." I paused a moment before asking, "But now that I think of it, where was your chauffeur on the night she died?"

"With me. We went to the Whitefish Club for dinner and a show after. He was with me the entire time."

The look I gave him had him adding. "James makes a good companion, and I don't like dining alone."

"I see. Mind if I ask where you found him?"

"From an agency. His references were all good, and he checked out just fine. What do you think he would have wanted with the vixen?"

I shrugged my shoulders at the obvious response. "If you can tell me where I can reach him, I'll ask."

"I sent him to the cemetery with a brass name plate with instructions to supervise its instillation. I assume that he will be out there all day."

"This is at the Island Cemetery, right?"

"Yes, I doubt if there is another one within a hundred miles."

I knew of a few, but I wasn't about to contradict him. The amount it cost for burials was astronomical. When you considered how many predators walked the streets, most preferred the low-cost necessity of the processing plants to keep civilization going. Especially the herbivores.

Saying goodbye, I took my hat from the butler and headed toward the cemetery. Once there, the gatekeeper showed me a map of where everything was and even volunteered to give me a tour. I turned him down. Walking through a field of desiccated meat was bad enough without a running commentary.

The construction was a big affair. Right on top of the hill for everyone to see, Greek columns surrounded the building along with the peaked roof. Above bronze doors, engraved in stone, were the family's name and their three-feathered crest. Caron-Grant was going all out with trimmings to spare.

I heard James Freely before I saw him. He was arguing with the workers, or maybe I should say threatening them. Instead of his spiffy suit, he had on his chauffeur uniform. I couldn't detect a bulge where a gun might be hidden.

Curious to see if I was right about the owner of the comb, I slid it across the walk toward his feet. The wait felt like forever. When he kicked it and realized what it was, his hands went to his pockets. The hyena then picked it up, brushed it off, and ran it through his fur.

I almost growled in satisfaction. Instead I said, "Why are you always giving everyone a hard time, Freely?"

15

Freely growled at me. I could see it in his eyes, the realization that he didn't have his gun. From the motion of his hands toward his pockets, I figured he had a knife at least. I lamented the fact that my coat was going to end up back at the tailor's. I didn't have my gun either, and it's a lot easier to fix a good coat than sliced flesh.

"What were you looking for at the vixen's place?"

The hyena didn't even bother to deny it. The next thing I knew, he had the blade out of his pocket and made a go for me. I used my jacket to blind him temporarily and avoided getting skewered. On his second pass I managed to get the knife tangled in the coat and out of his hand. That's when he tried his fists.

Freely managed to get in a few good licks before I took him to the ground with an arm behind his back.

"Who was she, Freely? Or I'll break your arm."

"I don't know."

"Who was she?" I yanked his arm up just shy of breaking it, and he screamed in pain.

"Just some whore. She stole some pics. I was trying to get them back."

"Explain."

"They were just photos. The guy was paying off, but before I could hand them over, she stole them."

"Who was she?"

"I don't know, I don't know." Once again Freely fainted.

I let him go, got up, and looked around. The two construction workers, one stork and one bull, were looking at me with big grins on their faces. The stork pointed over to a tent where a fresh grave waited for its new occupant, and the bull burst out laughing. He laughed even harder when I obliged and dropped Freely into the hole and walked off.

CHAPTER 3

By the time I got back to the city, the rain was coming down in buckets. I changed my suit, grabbed some lunch, and drove straight for the office. Duke was there waiting for me.

"This is a surprise. Usually, I'm the one coming to your office."

"Maybe I should come around more often. Velvet makes good company."

Before I could get territorial, Velvet asked, "Are you going to tell us what brought you here? I'm dying of curiosity."

"We found who killed your Arctic fox."

Every nerve ending was alive. I wanted to shake the identity of the killer out of Duke so that I could hand out my own brand of justice. Only, Duke's words dowsed everything worse than the rain outside.

"It was a young buck with a brand new license and driving over the limit. He might have run, but his mother found out and marched him right into the station."

"Are you certain?"

"We looked over everything again. Everything fits. As for the weird brake, things happen."

"What about her name?"

"We're still working on that." Duke's eyes narrowed. "What's up? You still think there's something fishy about her death?"

"Yes. I want to see her body."

Duke gave me another one of his looks before agreeing. "Okay, let's go to the morgue."

On our way out the door, I told Velvet to knock off early.

The morgue was cold, and the air was filled with the smell of blood and meat. The quiet was what got under your skin and made you jumpy. Duke asked a buzzard working there for the list of Frost's personal belongings. He handed me the list, and I read through it as we walked the halls on the way to see the body. Other than her new clothes there were only the usual items females carry. Lipstick, comb, and some money.

The buzzard pulled open a door in the unidentified section, and there the vixen was, looking as if she were asleep.

Not seeing any cuts, I asked, "They haven't done the autopsy yet?"

"No, just the x-ray for her neck. Now that we know what happened, there won't be an autopsy."

In my gut, I knew something wasn't right. Then I noticed it. The ring was gone. A thief would have taken both her money and anything of value. Frost wasn't robbed. I checked the list of belongings again before handing it to Duke.

"What now? What are they going to do with her body?"

"They'll hold her the usual time before processing the body."

"She's not being processed without a name."

"They can't hold every unidentified body, Kaiser."

"I'll pay the storage fee if I have to. She's not going without a name."

Duke and I parted ways, and I drove back to my apartment to find the post-pigeon had delivered me a letter from the dead. Frost must have looked up my address from an old listing. The pigeon had crossed out her swirling scrip and scratched in my new address.

With shaking hands, I opened it to read the note inside.

Dear Kaiser,

Today is such a wonderful day, and you helped make it that way. To say thank you isn't enough. When we met, I was at my breaking point. You've given me new hope. Until you, there was no one I could trust, but I feel I can trust you. Someday I may need your trust again. Until then, thank you.

Your Arctic fox.

Frustrated, I crushed the paper in my fist. Why couldn't she have lived? Why couldn't she have given me her real name?

A few beers later, I smoothed out the letter on the table and studied it. It wasn't a letter the usual streetwalker would write. There was none of the hard tones that seep in and grow in a person who knows the street. No, Frost's elegant script and wording showed she had class.

She had a name. I just needed to find it.

Impatient for an answer, I decided to find a weasel I knew by the name of Jordy. I found him sitting at a bar in his neck of the woods.

"Hello, Jordy."

"Buzz off."

Not wanting to waste time, I grabbed him by the neck and made sure he got a good view of my fangs.

"Okay, okay, geez, Kaiser, you don't have to get all sore."

I dropped him back on his seat and ordered a beer. After downing half, I asked, "The Arctic fox that was murdered, who was she?"

Jordy gave me a blank look. "Murdered? But..." Not wanting to see my teeth again he nodded. "Murdered."

The way his eyes darted around the bar made it

obvious the little pimp was scared.

"You working for an outfit or yourself, Jordy? Is that why you're scared?"

"No outfit, just myself. And your dame was not the female anyone wanted to be around. If I hadn't a dropped her for standing up customers, my neck might a ended up in a noose." Jordy rubbed his neck and looked sideways at me. "She was hot."

"Who said?"

"Don't know, and I don't want to know. Maybe some wannabe gunslinger wanted her as a steady. The word went out, and her traffic disappeared."

"And?"

"I said, I don't know."

When I growled and licked my teeth, Jordy got talkative again. "There's a house she used to work at." He muttered the address and slugged down his drink.

I let him alone and walked back to my car to think before heading to the address Jordy gave me. The place turned out to be a burnt-out shell of a wooden building. A husky pup saw me staring at the wreckage and said, "Somebody flipped a cigarette in the trash. It caught everything on fire and killed the females inside."

I fished in my pockets for a quarter and handed it to the pup. By the way his tail wagged, you would have thought it was a hundred-dollar bill. With the trail gone, I stopped in the nearest bar to drown my sorrows.

One beer down, I used the bar's payphone to call Duke and got him on the first try. "I need information about a fire." I gave Duke the address along with the number I was calling from and hung up. He wasn't long in getting back with me. The payphone rang, and I grabbed the handset before the bartender could.

"Kaiser here."

"The fire happened two weeks ago and was declared accidental. Some kid tossed a butt into the trash. The building was supposed to be condemned, but that didn't keep people out of it. Seven females died in the fire. Seems the flames blocked the front entrance and trash sealed the back door. The place went up like a tinderbox. What are you up to, Kaiser?"

"I'm still looking for her name."

"The fox? We found it, Lilian Seadrift. She used several different first names but the name Lilian she used the most, so that's the name we're going with."

"Are you sure?"

"There are a lot of cops on the force, Kaiser. A couple of patrol-hounds ran down the name." Duke let out a sigh before continuing. "We have the person who hit her and found a witness that said they saw her staggering drunk about a half block from where she was hit."

"Have you found her family yet?"

"No, but she did a good job of covering her tracks. We may never find them."

"Do not send her to the processing plant."

"Don't worry, Kaiser, we're not in a hurry and the morgue hasn't run out of room."

After growling a goodbye, I hung up the phone. The fox's name ran through my head, and I must have spoken it aloud. The snow leopard down at the end of the bar glared at me through glassy eyes. The red dress she wore plunged down to her belt buckle and the slit in her skirt did the same.

"Lilian… everybody's looking for Lilian. No one has any time for Sasha.

"Who's trying to find Lilian?"

The snow leopard was having trouble staying upright. "I liked Lilian, but she's gone, dead." She looked at me with whisky-drowned eyes. "Can't Sasha keep you company?"

CHAPTER 4

The bull of a bartender gave me a hard glare after I sat down next to Sasha. A good look at my teeth sent him shuffling down to the other end of the bar.

Sasha uncrossed a pair of gorgeous legs and nearly slid into my arms. "Oops."

"Looks like you might need to sober up a bit. Want to go for a ride?"

"Sure."

Not only did I have to help Sasha to the car but pour her into it. With the windows rolled down, she lounged in the passenger seat. Neither of us were in any hurry, so I meandered from street to street. Sasha fell asleep. When I got tired of driving, I parked somewhere around Rockaway Point. I turned the radio on low so as not to disturb her and settled in to wait.

Sasha woke up about an hour later. Curiosity was the only thing I could see in her eyes. "Do you have a name?"

"Kaiser Wrench. I take it yours is Sasha."

"Yes."

"Hope you like the beach."

She glanced out the windshield and then stretched that beautiful body of hers. The word distracting was the understatement of the year.

"It's still dark out."

"Do you want me to take you home?" I looked out at the moonlit sand. Not only did I need information, but Sasha had me intrigued. "Perhaps you prefer a walk?"

"Should I take off my shoes?"

"Go ahead. Take off anything you like."

She gave me a dreamy look and slipped out of the car. We strolled down the narrow lane, and she held my hand like she didn't want to ever let go. The moonlight danced over the white in her fur, turning her into an ethereal creature. We walked in silence past the wooden jetties until there was nothing but a long stretch of sand.

We sat down near the dunes and she shivered.

"You're cold. Here, take my coat."

"Thank you, this dress isn't very warm."

Her comment had my mind racing. I might have regretted handing over my coat if it wasn't for the fact her skirt refused to cover her legs.

"Do you have any cigarettes?" she asked.

"Sure." I lit two and handed her one.

"Thanks." Sasha inhaled and blew out the smoke as she looked at me sideways. "You wanted to know about Lilian. You do know she's dead, right?"

"What I want to know is who killed her. And before you ask, I'm a private investigator."

"So, you think she was murdered? That it wasn't a hit and run."

"I'm not sure what to think."

"It was murder." Sasha took another drag and shook her head. "It has to be."

"Care to enlighten me?" When she didn't answer right away, I asked, "How did you know Lilian?"

Sasha shifted her pose and nearly distracted me from what we were talking about. Even with my coat over her shoulders, she didn't bother to use it to shield the neckline of her dress.

23

"Let's just say we worked together, and not just at the house which burnt down."

"You look too classy for that area."

"But not so smart." Sasha wrote two letters in the sand. V.D. "I had it all until I messed up and no one wanted me anymore. I finally wised up and went to the hospital. The house burnt down while I was there."

"Anyone can get into the business and make money. The trouble is, the ending is all the same."

"True enough. But getting paid for it seemed better than giving it away. And I had a stupid idea that what was good for the goose is good for the gander. More fool me." She looked at me sideways and took another drag on her cigarette. "I met someone who hooked me up with a room and a phone number. Everything was grand until I screwed up, and it all went south. Lilian had her reasons for being there. Not the same as mine, but there was something."

"Why were you at the bar?"

"Getting drunk and mourning my friend. Then you showed up. Sorry about making a pass at you."

"I'm not."

Sasha smiled but continued to talk. "Lilian was in the racket before I joined. Some females find a male that marries them, and they get out. Others take the slow drive down the hill and end up in the houses or on the streets. The strange thing about Lilian was she quit suddenly without an explanation. But instead of getting out of the business, she used the street to hide. Lilian was scared. Of what, I don't know, but she was scared."

Recalling Lilian's ransacked apartment, I asked, "Did she have anything worth steeling?"

"No. But then, she could be secretive. She did have a camera. An imported thing she used for a previous job. Something that she could use to take pictures of couples on the street. They'd send a quarter in with the card she'd pass them, and they'd get a memento of the fun time they were having."

"Was this a recent job?"

"No." Sasha's brow furrowed in thought. "She still had a few of the cards. Photo Fast was the name of the company."

"What's your full name?"

"Sasha Berlin, from a little town in the back of beyond." She looked down at her claws. "My mother thinks I'm a model."

"Does the name James Freely mean anything to you?"

She shook her head. "No."

Stymied, I looked out at the ocean.

"Kaiser, did you love Lilian?"

"I only met her once, but it felt like she was a friend. And I don't like it when friends die."

Sasha lost her cigarette and snuggled up closer. "I don't suppose we could be friends?"

She was all warm kisses and soft fur.

The alarm clock didn't wake me the next morning, but the phone sure did. Velvet was on the other end of the line.

"Kaiser, where are you? Carousing I suppose?"

"I…"

"We got a client in the office, and I mean big client. As in Lucius Caron-Grant himself. His appointment is at two. I suggest you wash the lipstick out of your fur before you see him. Wear the dark blue tie, not that awful green one."

"Did he have anyone with him?"

"No. Why?"

"Just checking. I'll be there in a bit." I rang off and cleaned up. The suit I had on yesterday was a mess. The only other outfit I had available was a tweed tailored to fit my gun, and the suit didn't fit right without it. I managed to get to the offices a good fifteen minutes before Caron-Grant.

Velvet buzzed me on the switch box as soon as he

arrived. "A Mr. Lucius Caron-Grant is here to see you."

"Send him in."

When the old fox walked in, I got up and shook his hand. "Nice to see you again, Mr. Caron."

"Likewise."

Lucius Caron-Grant had a cane with him today, and when he sat down, he had a thoughtful expression on his face. "I've been thinking about that female you told me about."

"The Arctic fox? Lilian Seadrift was her name."

"That's wonderful. Has her family been informed?"

"That's another search of a haystack."

"Oh, dear. That sounds like a lot of work."

"It is."

"Why don't I hire you to find them?"

"Excuse me? I mean, I was going to poke around anyway…"

"But this way you get paid for it." Caron smiled at me like it was the brightest thing he'd ever come up with. "I'm always financing some charity, why not help you in your search for this vixen's family?"

"That would be great. Thank you."

Caron pulled out his wallet and handed me enough cash to keep me searching full time for three weeks. "If you find them sooner, consider the rest a bonus."

"That's very generous of you Mr. Caron."

"Nonsense, I know what it's like to be totally alone. My wife died in a boating accident, and my only son died in the first world war. Even his daughter is lost to me." He leaned closer, and his sly grin returned. "I looked you up, Mr. Wrench. You're quite the character, and an honorable male."

I wasn't sure what things he heard, but the compliment did have me squirming in my chair. "Would you like the reports sent to your house on Long Island?"

"Yes, that will be fine."

We rose from our chairs, and I asked, "Oh, is James

Freely still working for you?"

"No. At the moment, my gardener is driving me until I find a suitable replacement."

We said our goodbyes, and I walked him to the door.

When I turned around, Velvet gave me a toothy grin. That's when I noticed her end of the intercom box was switched on, so she could eavesdrop. I picked up the handset of her phone and called Duke.

"Hey, Duke. How about we get a cup of coffee and a doughnut?"

"Am I going to regret this?"

"I'll see you at the Mocha Moose."

He growled an affirmative and hung up.

By the time I made it to the beanery, Duke was already sitting in the back corner. After the waiter took our order, I asked Duke, "Tell me how the call-female racket works in this town."

His ears went back, and he gave me a nasty snarl to which I raised my hands.

"I'm not going to bust your chops. I need information."

"That's a loaded question. If I say what I know, I look crooked. If I say I don't know anything, I look like an idiot."

"And neither of us is so uptight as to think we could ever stop that kind of business. The bureaucrats would do better making it legal and taxing the income. They'd make a fortune."

Duke gave me one of his longsuffering sighs. "Customers aren't going to complain to the police when they get stiffed, but we know what's going on. Most of the time our hands are tied by the law and other times by political pressure. Evidence is a pain to find. The big guys don't keep the houses, and their books are hidden. The females get their cut, but it's not wise to complain about the amount."

"They get roughed up?"

"More like interesting suicides. Roman Chase was the only one not in that category. Chase ran a bunch of houses and made too much of a stink. We found him down an alley shot full of holes. And not one stool pigeon would talk."

I scratched my chin and asked, "You said interesting suicides? What's that supposed to mean?"

"Murder, plain and simple."

Duke didn't need to interpret my grin.

"You can be such a bastard, Kaiser. I suppose you're still on your kick about Lilian Seadrift?"

"If the box fits."

We ate our doughnuts in silence for a bit.

"Lilian Seadrift was hit by a car. No other person was hurt in that area that night. The deer was drunk, so he can't even give us a description of the person he hit. Plus, we found traces on the car bumper."

"You're wrong, Duke. Lilian was murdered. I can't tell you how I know, and I don't have proof yet. But I will. Do you know who's the pimp behind the curtain?"

"We don't know for sure, just a few suspects."

"I'll start with those first."

"Not before you tell me what you know."

We ordered more coffee, and I started at the beginning. By the time we finished our cups, Duke knew everything I did.

"Lilian was killed for a reason," said Duke.

"Yeah, but was the reason from something before the racket or during?"

"Blackmail?"

"Doesn't feel right. Plus, Lilian wasn't stupid."

"What about James Freely? How does he fit into this?"

I shook my head, but even I couldn't figure how Freely came into this mess. "I can see him blackmailing someone. But Lilian's death showed too much finesse. Freely is nothing more than a common thug."

"And your client?"

"Caron-Grant might be going loopy in his old age, but he seems all right. He dumped Freely when I told him what happened."

"What about Sasha Berlin?"

"What about her? Sasha was Lilian's friend and wised up before it was too late."

Duke rubbed his face and looked as frustrated as I felt. "Okay, why is the guy at the diner and Jordy scared?"

"If we knew that, we probably wouldn't be sitting here banging our heads against the wall. Now, who do you suspect?"

"What I have is suspicions, and I'm not giving you those to go off half-cocked. What I will give you is the names I do know for certain. They're small fish, but like I said, finding evidence is tough."

"Fine. I'll take what I can get."

With ears back, Duke leaned closer. "So, what else do you what from me?"

"Work Lilian's case like a murder. Something is bound to come up."

"And?"

"And what? I got a date with Sasha. Should I ask her if she has a friend?"

CHAPTER 5

Sasha's apartment was over on West Fifty-Sixth. She must have caught me wrinkling my nose at the smell of fresh paint.

"It's a new place. There were too many memories in the old one." She smiled and announced, "I've got a new job modeling at a department store." She struck a pose and walked around the small living area as if she were modeling an expensive gown instead of the plain black number she had on. Truth be told, Sasha could have worn burlap and made it appealing.

"Will anyone from your past give you problems?"

"Doubtful. I'm not like Lilian. She was constantly running into people she knew. If anyone does think they remember me, I can always play dumb. Act like they're mistaken."

Sasha made us a couple of drinks and sat down on the couch next to me. "Are you..." The happy confidence disappeared, replaced by insecurity. "I do like you..."

"I'm not here for that."

"Good." She relaxed and a shy smile touched her lips. "With what happened, and well, I wasn't sure what to think."

"That was my fault. Would you like to start over?"

"If you don't mind."

"I'll do my best to behave."

Sasha laughed at that, but she sobered with my next comment.

"Lilian was murdered, but I can't prove it. With the things you know, do you think you can help me?"

"I don't want to go back."

"I'm not asking you to." I wrapped an arm around her and pulled her close. "Do you think Lilian could be a blackmailer?"

"No. This might sound a little strange, but Lilian was honorable. Why she was in the business, I don't know. It could have been the money. Maybe she was looking for a rich husband. Some do and succeed. Lilian didn't drink, smoke, and never did drugs. But she was... driven. There was something she was after, but I never found out what that something was."

Tired of running in circles, I asked, "Tell me about the call-female racket."

Every muscle in her body tensed. "Please, Kaiser, no. They'll kill me if they find out I said anything. They'll kill you. These are nasty people. A person's life doesn't mean anything to them. More than one person has died by making that mistake."

Sasha shifted in my embrace so that she could look me in the eye. "These people are tight-knit and organized. If anyone tries to go out on their own, they get put down and fast. Millions are raked in, and if you don't hand over your cut, they cut you. Do not mess with these people."

"Everything has a weakness, even predators can be prey. When it comes to bad guys, they might prey on your regular citizen, but I'm the predator they run from. As for you, don't worry. They're not going to know you breathed a word."

We drank our drinks in silence, and Sasha refilled the glasses. She studied me as she returned to the couch.

31

"The male at the top is a mystery. Perhaps it's more than one. The thing is, it's organized. The females are brought in by invitation only and must meet certain criteria. Remember what I said about a few marrying? That doesn't happen if a female speaks like a gutter rat or can't figure out what fork to use at a dinner party. Beauty, education, and decorum is their holy trinity."

Sasha studied her claws for a moment before continuing. "The clients are well off. An appointment could be on a yacht, a party, or any number of high-class events you can think of, public or private. And since the female has already been seen around town with too many males before being inducted into the racket, no one says boo."

The embarrassment of the memory must have gotten to her because she refused to look me in the eye as she talked.

"After being investigated, the female is approached about getting paid for what she's doing. On acceptance, she's given an apartment and her name is placed in a book as a certain type. Gifts can be kept but the money's handled by someone else up front, and the female gets a cut deposited into the bank. If a female wants to leave, she can any time and for any reason. Like marrying a rich male. If she keeps her mouth shut. And they will. God forbid someone finds out what they were, their social standing would crumble."

The ice cubes in the bottom of her glass suddenly became interesting, and it was some time before she decided to go on.

"A female needs to keep clean though. When my appointments dried up, one of the other females told me why. Someone complained. So, I sold my apartment and ended up working in one of the houses. Lilian convinced me to go to the hospital and get clean, that I didn't need to be ashamed."

I took her glass and put it on the table before pulling

her back into my arms. Sasha buried her face in my chest but didn't cry.

I said, "I need a name."

"Marlow Press owns a few night clubs, but he's always at the Malibu Club. Press won't have the main records, but he might have temporary ones. But even those would be kept hidden."

She shifted to her knees and looked me straight in the eye. "Be careful. Please, Kaiser, I…"

"What's your worry, I will."

"I can't help it. You're… you're just so easy to get hung up on."

"So are you."

Sasha's kiss was as sweet as honey, and if I wasn't careful, I'd break my promise to behave.

After a few more smoldering kisses, I managed to make it to the door and headed straight for Malibu Club.

The Malibu Club was parked in a cellar with only a neon sign to advertise its whereabouts. I tipped the doorman the usual quarter and entered the place. Through the cloud of cigarette smoke, I could tell the place was high-end. There was no tinsel and glitz. The bar was solid mahogany and set along one wall, while tables lined a nice size dance floor. The patrons of the place weren't local, at least not the males. A half dozen hostesses moved among the crowd, making certain everyone enjoyed themselves.

I took a table in the far corner and ordered a drink. Not long after, one of the hostesses sauntered my way. Otters have that cute way of wiggling when they walk that makes you want to smile, and I'm not immune.

"How are you doing tonight?"

I pulled a chair out for her, and after glancing around, she decided to take a load off. She looked me up and down as I ordered her a drink and another for myself.

"You don't look like a farmer."

Not wanting to waste time, I figured I'd get down to business. "I'm not. But I am looking for Marlow. Is he in?"

"Marlow never gets in before midnight. Are you two friends, or can the manager help you?"

"Not really and no. This is something I need to talk to him about. Do you remember a Lilian Seadrift?"

The hostess set her glass down. "Lilian is dead."

"Yeah, she is. Do you know where she lived?"

"Why?"

"Because Lilian Seadrift is a phony name. And insurance investigators have a nose for smelling lies. If she is who I think she is, I've got a nice size policy I'd like to deal with and get out of my fur. The beneficiaries wouldn't mind lining their pockets either."

"Why are you looking around here?"

"Didn't she work here?"

The hostess glanced away. "Lilian worked at a house."

"The house burnt down a few weeks ago, and I already checked her temporary digs. Where was she before then?"

"I don't know. When she left here, I lost track of her. Though a few people saw her around."

"There's a reward."

"For her identity?"

"For good information, like where she lived before. There's one too many phony claims to deal with and too few untampered witnesses to identify her."

"So, in other words, keep my mouth shut, if, and when I find anything. How much?"

Hoping I was on to something, I pulled a number out of the air. "Five bills." The money was half what Caron-Grant had paid me, but if the information was good, it would be worth the loss. The sparkle of greed in her eyes was all I needed to know she was hooked.

"Come back soon, and I'll see what I can do." She smiled, finished her drink, and returned to her job.

Five after midnight, the bartenders hustled a little faster, and the patrons started throwing greetings around. Marlow Press walked through the door.

Marlow Press turned out to be a short, squat beaver. With large front teeth and a perpetual smile, he was not someone you'd expect to be a tough guy. Unlike the two gorillas in tuxedos that flanked him, the beaver looked like everybody's favorite uncle.

The trio made their way past the crowd and exited through an alcove.

After giving him time to settle in, I paid my check and headed after them. In the hallway past the alcove were two doors. One marked exit and an unmarked steel barrier.

When I pressed a button in the jamb of the steel door, I didn't hear the bell, but the door was opened by one of the apes.

"I'm here to see Marlow Press. Is he available?"

"Name?"

"Sweeny Dale from Kansas."

The gorilla glared at me but made a call from a phone mounted on the wall. When he hung up, he motioned me through into a short hallway. The sound proofing was top dollar because when the door closed behind me, I couldn't hear a thing from the party going on outside. The ape motioned me to the other door.

I hurried through and was just in time to see the back door to the room I entered close. Marlow Press sat at his desk, and the other ape rested on a sofa. Signed pictures of famous actors hung on the wall, but no bookshelves or indication of a safe.

"Mr. Press?"

"Yes. And you are Mr. Dale. Please, do sit down."

The gorilla shifted in his seat. "He's packing, boss."

"Good eye," I said. "Kansas cop. Never leave home without it."

"Yes. Well, what can I do for you?"

"We've got a convention in town next month and need some females to help with the party. I hear you're the beaver to see."

Press showed no reaction other than confusion. "How

very strange."

"Look, some of the guys came home from vacation and spread your praise. What can I say?"

"They must have gotten me confused with someone else. Sorry."

"That's all right. Sorry to take up your time."

The apes let me out the same way I came in. Not wanting to stay in the joint any longer, I took up surveillance in a café down the street. Part way through a Danish, I spotted Press stepping out onto the street alone.

The amusing thing was, I tailed him to the same parking garage I stashed my own jalopy. I gave the attendant my ticket, and he handed me my keys. There were the usual sounds of a parking garage, shoes on gravel, doors shutting, and engines turning over.

A weak cry from between a row of cars had me running toward the spot. More fool me. The butt end of a gun cracked my skull and had me flat on my face. There was no time and no room to stop the beating I got. Before I blacked out, I heard someone say, "That's enough... I said that's enough. Let's go."

CHAPTER 6

The rays of morning sunlight woke me. Snorting gravel is not how I wanted to start the day, and I cursed myself for running into the trap. Stiff, sore, and aching all over, I managed to prop myself up against the car nearest to me. The goons left me my wallet and my gun, but my pride had taken a bigger beating than my body.

How long I sat there until I noticed something shiny in the gravel, I don't know. Shifting, I forced myself through the aches, and not only picked up the shiny object, but stood up. In my hand, I held a gold ring with a blue fleur-de-lis. Lilian's ring.

"Hello, beautiful."

With a smile plastered on my face, I staggered to my own car and drove out of the parking lot. The route home was hampered by the pain that shot through my body. Just using the pedals was a chore. Somehow, I managed to make it to Sasha's place. Leaving the jalopy out front, I climbed the steps and almost used my face to knock on the door, I was teetering so bad.

Sasha answered the door and got the shock of a lifetime. "Kaiser, what happened?"

I growled in response.

"Let's get you inside, and I'll call a doctor."

"No doctor."

"But—"

"I'll be fine."

I staggered to the couch and sat down. Sasha took off my shoes and checked me over before I could protest.

"I have some time before I need to get to work. Do you want me to call in?"

"No. You need the job. Just let me rest, and I'll get out of your fur."

"You're lucky I was a nurse's aide during the war." Sasha proved her point by getting me out of my shirt, tie, and coat with a deft hand. With a basin of water and washcloth, she cleaned my cuts and brushed out my fur without a whimper. Before I knew it, my pants and socks were on the clothes pile, and I was stretched out on the couch.

Somewhere along the line I fell asleep. When I woke up, Sasha was gone, but she left a note.

Dear Kaiser,

Rest up, I'll be back with a change of clothes for you. I checked your wallet for your address and have your keys. Your gun is under the sofa.

Love, Sasha.

Next to the note was my wallet, change, and the ring.

The phone was in arm's reach, thankfully. I dialed the operator then asked for information. Once I gave them Caron-Grant's name and address, they rang me through. The butler answered, and I had to wait for him to find his boss. Caron-Grant's cheery voice answered.

"Hello, Mr. Wrench. How are things?"

"Not so hot. I fell for a sucker's trap and got my clock cleaned."

"Are you all right?"

"I'll be fine. They didn't scare me. If anything, Press' goons did me a good turn. One of them killed the Arctic fox."

"Really?"

"Yeah, he dropped her ring, and I've got it now. The bad thing is that I didn't see the guy who dropped it. Things happened a bit too fast."

"I see. Perhaps I shouldn't have encouraged you."

"Nonsense. I'd have gotten here on my own. I just wanted to check in with you. Everything's fine, and I'll let you know what else I find."

"Yes. Please do."

The next call I made was to Duke. While I told him about everything but the ring, he still knew I was holding out on him.

"And?"

"And what?"

"You have that, cat in the cream, tone in your voice."

"That's because I'm getting somewhere. Press' goons may or may not have been the ones who got to me, but there was someone else. Someone who was leaving when I came in the room. I didn't see them, but it's possible they were the ones responsible. Whoever it was wanted to finish me off. Press called him off. Seeing as he needs to keep his nose clean, I don't think he wanted to chance even a hint of a murder charge."

"Well, lady luck is still shining on you. The kid who hit your vixen was insured. The company wants to pay off and is hell bent on finding her relatives. I didn't say a word about what you hood-winked me into, but right now they're looking into your pal James Freely. The guy is from out west. On paper, he's clean and has only been fingerprinted for his gun license. But I phoned a few officers from his old haunts, and they say he had a rep with the lowlifes out there. A regular gunslinger with an itchy trigger finger."

"He's no longer working for Caron-Grant."

"Freely turned in his gun and license when he was let go. Let's hope he keeps away from knives."

"Sorry to disappoint you, but he's not bad with a

knife."

Duke's growl came over the line, but I ignored it and told him I needed to get some sleep. With the vixen's ring secured on my pinky finger, I took another nap and didn't wake up until Sasha came home.

"Are you feeling better?" Sasha felt my forehead. "You don't feel like you have a fever."

"I'm fine. Stiff, but fine."

"Why don't you take a warm shower while I make dinner? It might help."

"Sounds great." I wrapped the sheet around me and grabbed my clothes. "Have I told you how beautiful you are?"

The question put a smile on her face. She playfully pulled at the sheet wrapped around me, and I hustled into the bathroom before it got into a full-scale tug of war.

After a hot shower, I got dressed. Sasha had pork chops with all the trimmings when I stepped into the kitchen. After we ate, we discussed the case over pie and still came up with the same questions, if not more.

"What can I do to help," asked Sasha.

"Use your noggin. Think about all the conversations you had with Lilian. Try to remember everything. The smallest thing can lead to something big. And whatever you do, don't go gallivanting out on your own. I don't want you ending up on someone's trouble list."

"Do you like me that much?"

"Honey, I like you lots. You're one heck of a gem. I think…"

Sasha's eyes filled with tears. "Don't. Don't say it. I… I don't think I could handle it right now."

"Anything you want, Honey."

The kiss made my fur stand on end, and I was feeling no pain. Reluctantly, we pulled apart, and I grabbed my hat. I was out the door before I could change my mind.

CHAPTER 7

When I got down to my car, I found a parking ticket under the windshield wiper. I pulled it out and shoved it in the glove box to deal with later.

Lilian's ring glowed on my pinky finger in the waning light as if teasing me.

I started the car and pulled into traffic. The ring was a clue I needed information on and fast.

When I reached downtown, a lot of the smaller shops were closed. The jewelry shop I needed to find was run by an old friend of mine. I almost drove right by the place.

I parallel parked and bolted for the shop door. All the lights were off, and the shades pulled. Dani lived above the shop, but there was always a chance he went out for the evening. When the shades moved and a bird's eye peeked out at me, I had to smile.

Dani had the door unlocked and opened in seconds. With a flourish of his black and white wings the magpie welcomed me into his shop. "Good evening, Kaiser. What brings you to my humble shop at this hour?"

"I need help with a ring."

"Are you getting married?" Dani looked at me cockeyed as he closed and locked the door behind me.

41

"No. I'm working on a case." I held up my hand with the ring still on my finger. "It belonged to a dead vixen."

The magpie's eyes lit up, and he wiggled his feathery fingers for me to hand the ring over. "Will I be helping to bait a trap for a crook again?"

"Right now, I just need information. What can you tell me about this thing?"

Dani pulled a jeweler's glass out of his vest and stuck it in his eye. He took the ring and examined it for several minutes, turning it over more than once.

The jeweler's glass dropped from his eye and into his hand. He tucked the glass back into his vest as he handed me back the ring. "It's an antique. Does it have a history?"

"No."

"Too bad. I've seen many similar rings. Family heirlooms. What I can tell you is that it is most likely a female's ring and has never been inscribed. Or if it has, the inscription has long been worn away. The composition of metal used to make that ring is very sturdy but not so nice to look at. That's why it's not used today. People like things to be pretty and shiny."

His head waggled back and forth as he hummed in thought.

"Perhaps three hundred years old. Yes, three hundred at least. Which means it was brought from the old country. Where? Good question. With the war, so many records were destroyed. And the Nazis..." His eyes narrowed, and he grew silent for a moment before he shook himself and returned to the subject at hand. "But even if they hadn't been, this ring..." Dani pointed at the ring now back on my pinky, "was custom made by a small family jeweler. Record of its commission may have existed, but it's unlikely."

"What about the emblem?"

"It is very worn, but no, that is all I can tell you."

"You've saved me a lot of legwork. Thanks."

We said our goodbyes, and I got back in my car. The

ring was another dead end, or was it? There had to be something significant about it, or the killer wouldn't have removed it from the body.

An idea struck me, and I did a U-turn and headed back to the carpark where I got jumped. Press might have been able to spot a phony and tried warning me off, but they didn't know who I was. If they had, they probably would have made sure I was dead.

When I got to the parking lot, I knocked on the attendant's window and the owl slid it open. "Yes?"

"Did anybody lose anything in the lot lately?"

"Just car keys. Have you checked the ads in the newspaper?"

"I'll do that."

On the way back to my car, I couldn't help doing a bit of reconnaissance. The lot was dark, but every time a car pulled in, the head lights would sweep the area. When I noticed movement in the all-night parking section where I got jumped, I hunkered down and did some stalking. Whoever it was who jumped me wasn't going to get a second chance.

The canine was so intent on his search he didn't even hear me come up behind him.

"Lose something?"

He lost his footing on the gravel when he tried standing up and ended up falling on his face. That didn't keep him from coming up swinging. I blocked his punch and clocked him right in the jaw. The canine staggered back, and I crowded him in order to finish the job. Once he was out cold, I lit a match to check who he was. His smell wasn't familiar.

The guy was some sort of African wild dog. I'd bloodied his snout but good. When I patted him down, I didn't find a gun or a set of keys. The thought that I just roughed up a guy trying to find his keys didn't sit well with me, but on the other hand, he did make the first swing.

The hand-tooled Moroccan leather wallet he had was

stuffed full of cash. His license identified him as Darren Hutchins.

Irritated, I hopped the fence and figured I'd try my luck at the Malibu Club. The doorman was busy opening doors of taxis and picking up tips, enabling me to slip into the place unnoticed. Press and his goons weren't around, so I took a table in the back again.

The waiter came by with a drink, but before I could taste it, the otter from the other night was running her fingers through my fur. "I've been looking for you."

She parked her butt in the seat next to mine and leaned on my arm like she was flirting. Her eyes glittered with hunger. "You mentioned five hundred dollars. I think I've found what you want, but it'll cost you more than five."

"More?"

"Perhaps."

The singer on stage was coming to the end of her act, and the otter got jittery. "Leave before the lights go up. I get out of here at one, so I'll meet you on the corner. You got a car?"

I nodded in response.

"Then you'll be driving me home."

She left, and I didn't bother staying any longer.

I had quite a wait until I could pick her up. The bar a few blocks down the street was crowded but still had a stool to park my behind. The otter might be lying about what she found, but I figured it worth a chance. What galled me was that I might have to hand over more than half my earnings on this job. Granted, I was planning on doing it for free, but five hundred dollars can put a lot of steaks on the table.

It was my own fault, and I knew it. There was no going back. The thought of Caron-Grant popped in my head two hours later along with the thought of what he might say. Just on a hunch, I decided to report in.

At the risk of losing my seat, I headed to the back of the bar. The pay phone was located down the hall near the restrooms. One nickel got me the long distance operator, and she patched me through to Caron-Grant's home phone. The nickel was followed by several dimes. Partially because I had to argue with the naked mole-rat of a butler.

When Caron-Grant did get to the phone, he sounded sleepy. "Hello."

"Sorry to call you so late, Mr. Caron, but something's come up. Something important."

"Yes?"

"I might have a line on the vixen. I offered a female five hundred dollars for information. The problem is she wants more than just five. My question to you is, should I hand over the cash or go at it by another route?"

"What is this information?"

"Not sure. She wants me to meet her later."

"What are the odds that it's good information?"

"Plenty good. The female works as a hostess of the Malibu Club and knew Lilian a while back. That's where everything seems to be leading, somewhere in her past."

"Go ahead and write her a check, and I'll have the bank wire money into your account. Just call and let me know the amount."

"That's very generous of you, Mr. Caron."

"It's only money. Good luck, Mr. Wrench."

We said our goodbyes, and I returned to the bar. Just after midnight, I paid my bill and got a taxi to run me over to my car. By one o'clock I was cruising down the street and stopped at the corner where the otter stood waiting, holding an overnight bag.

"Good timing." She slipped into the passenger side, and we were off.

"Where are we going?"

"My place is on Eighty-Ninth."

"Okay." As I drove, I couldn't help glancing down at the bag at her feet. "You planning a trip?"

"Perhaps you could join me?" The look in her eyes had me wondering.

When I pulled up to her place and parked, I got out and opened her door. With the bag in one hand and the otter hanging onto the other, we entered her building.

The female's apartment was two flights up. A nice place, cozy, but with furniture too small and frail for me to sit in. I took my hat off, dropped the overnight bag she brought, and sat on the floor.

"We should introduce ourselves. I'm Adaline Marsh."

"Kaiser Wrench, and I'm not an insurance investigator, but a P.I."

"I already knew that."

"You did?"

"Uh-huh. I've seen your picture in the paper. Let me just say you look much better in person."

"Thanks."

Adaline stared at me for a long while before speaking. "Marlow Press is a louse. Do you know what he's up to?"

"Some. I also know the police can't cage him without evidence. What have you got against him?"

"I'm tired of watching him destroy people. He might pay my salary, but that doesn't mean I have to like him." She leaned back in her chair. "You got the dough?"

"Some. What are you going to do with it?"

"Get out of town. This city will rot you from the inside out. I can't stand it anymore."

I reached over and pulled the bag toward me. It was old, scuffed, and paint-splattered. I tried the catch, but it was locked. "Yours?"

"No. Lilian's. The thing was dumped in the prop room with a bunch of other garbage. There was a bus ticket with her name on it tied to the handle. Good question how long it's been there. At least since Marlow remodeled the place, and that was a while ago. All sorts of stuff got stashed in that room."

Adaline got up and sauntered to the kitchen. She came back with a bottle of wine and glasses. We sat and drank in silence. Adaline lounged in her chair with her legs curled up beneath her, letting me get a nice view of her shapely legs. The shoulders of her dress hung loose and tapered into a slim waist.

"Aren't you going to open it?"

"Do you have an ice pick? I'd hate to break a claw." Just to be silly, I held up my forefinger with the claw extended. Adaline took it as an invitation and had me in a lip lock that could set a house on fire.

When she came up for air, she gave me a wicked smile and booped my nose before darting into the kitchen. I heard her searching the drawers, but when the noise stopped, and she hadn't returned, I started to wonder what she was up to next.

I didn't have long to wait. Adaline came back into the room holding a small ice pick and wearing a silk robe. "Like it?"

"Very nice."

She handed me the ice pick and asked, "Can that thing wait?"

"Nope."

Using the tip of the ice pick, I jammed it underneath the clasp and popped the hasp. I tossed the ice pick on a side table, but before I could look in the bag, the light snapped off. The only light that came into the room was from a small lamp on the far side of the apartment.

"Kaiser?"

I turned and the roar I was going to give her caught in my throat. Adaline had tossed her robe on the couch and stood before me in high-heels and smoking a cigarette. The smile on her lips and the fire in her eyes held promises most males would willingly die for.

The next thing I knew, Adaline was in my arms and introducing me to things I didn't think were possible.

Adaline laughed when I fumbled for a cigarette.

"It's nice to be important to someone."

"You won't get an argument out of me. Have you finished distracting me, or can I get back to the case?"

She took another drag on her cigarette and motioned for me to do what I please.

I grabbed the case before she could change her mind and dumped it out on the floor. Baby clothes spilt out onto the floor. Every item was brand new. Some still had the price tag stuck on. I searched through the pockets and found nothing but safety pins. The lid pocket held an envelope of snapshots. In the pictures, a young, innocent Lilian stared back at me. A picnic, a beach, and other outings. In every shot she was smiling and happy. She also wore her ring.

The backgrounds gave me nothing. No landmark, not even a sign.

Adaline leaned over my shoulder to look. "Does any of this help you?"

"Maybe." An idea was coalescing in my mind. it wasn't complete, but it was there. I pulled out my check book. "What do I owe you?"

"Nothing." Adaline ran her quick little fingers through my fur. "You've already paid for it."

I wrote out the check anyway and handed it to her. "Then this is to help you get out of the city and set up someplace nice."

"I'll have to drop you a line on where to visit."

Once I had everything up off the floor and put back in place, bag in hand, I grabbed my hat and gave Adaline a wink. She winked back.

CHAPTER 8

There was no sleeping for me that night. I spent it staring at the contents of the bag spread over the kitchen table back at my apartment. The vixen was an enigma.

When the sun came up, I remembered to call Caron-Grant. This time he answered the phone and not the butler.

"Good morning, Mr. Wrench. How did everything go? Did you get any more information?"

"Nothing other than a bag full of more questions, baby clothes, and pictures. I haven't puzzled it out yet but I'll find something. This stuff might lead me somewhere."

"Baby clothes and..." Caron-Grant's voice trailed off in a mumble of words.

"I went ahead and turned over five hundred to the dame."

"Good, I'll arrange the wire transfer."

"Thanks."

After I rang off, I put everything back in the bag and went to bed. The next thing I knew, the phone was ringing like there was no tomorrow. When I answered it, the anger in Velvet's voice was tinged in relief.

"Hello, Kaiser? Where have you been? Do you have

any idea what time it is? I've been calling every bar in town trying to find you."

"Been sleeping here in my apartment."

"I called there. Several times."

"I was tired."

"Tired from your latest workout partner or passed out? Never mind. Duke called. It had to do with James Freely."

That had me awake and paying attention. "I'll call him now. Talk to you later."

I hit the cutoff bar on the phone base, took a breath, and dialed police headquarters. The dog at the desk said the captain had been in earlier but didn't know where he was now.

I hung up the phone and decided to get cleaned up. Halfway through my bath, I heard the phone ring and jumped out of the tub to answer it.

"Hello?"

Duke chuckled. "What kind of hours do you keep, Kaiser? It's almost one."

"Don't you know? I make my own. Velvet said you had information?"

"Yes. Well, one of the inquiries I sent out about James Freely came back and put him in a bad light. Seems he matches a description of someone wanted for murder. Only thing is, the witness is dead. I'll do some follow up, try to get more information, and let you know what I find. Right now, I'm dealing with a dead otter."

"Anyone interesting?"

"A hostess from the Malibu Club."

I swore and said, "Let me guess, suicide."

Duke didn't say anything for a full minute. "Please, do not tell me this one is murder."

"Was her name Adaline Marsh?"

"Yes."

"Is she at the morgue?"

"Yes." Duke's voice was turning into a growl.

"I'll meet you there in twenty."

When I got to the coroner's office, Duke was pacing the hallway. He took me straight to the body and flipped back the sheet. "This her?"

"Yes."

"Does she have a connection with the Seadrift case?"

"Yes."

"Damn it, Kaiser. The coroner is positive it's suicide."

"She was murdered."

Duke's tail drooped along with his ears. "Let's get something to eat and talk about this."

"I'm not hungry."

"Well, I am. Now let's go."

We stopped at a little Italian place down the street, and Duke ordered spaghetti. I settled for coffee.

"Tell me what you know, or think you know, Duke."

"Her name was Adaline Marsh. Worked for Marlow Press for five years. Ex-dancer. Ex-stripper. She lived in an upscale furnished apartment, and the super said she was a fine tenant. The last few months she's been down in the dumps. She left a suicide note."

"It's a fake."

"That's not what the Labrador said, and he's the expert on handwriting."

"Have him check it again."

Duke looked down at his meal and nodded.

"Fine." After eating another mouthful of spaghetti, he added, "We figure that around dawn, she walked down to the pier that's being dismantled over on River Drive. She left her hat, shoes, purse, everything in a neat pile and jumped in. Evidently she couldn't swim."

"Don't all otters swim?"

Duke shrugged. "Thought so, but apparently not. She'd been in the water four or five hours before a couple of cubs found her body."

"I left her place just before three. And trust me, Duke, she was smiling and alive when I left."

"There are days I really hate you. Is there a reason why

you were at her apartment in the wee hours of the morning? Other than the obvious, that is."

"Adaline found an overnight bag that belonged to Lilian. The bag was full of baby clothes and old vacation photos. She was poking around for information because I asked her to. Like I said, she was very happy when I left."

Duke checked his watch. "The coroner's doing the autopsy right now."

"He won't change his verdict."

Duke narrowed his eyes at me. "Get me proof."

"I'll get you proof. When I do, it'll be someone willing to purge their guts of all the information they have."

"You know what we're up against. These guys pay protection money to keep everything quiet."

"Since when have I cared who pays what or about keeping quiet?"

"Never. But we need to do this right or it'll be our necks."

Once Duke finished his meal, I said, "I don't have time for the legwork. Can you check the hospitals about Lillian and the possibility that she had a kit?"

"That's already on my list."

We said our goodbyes, and I set out for River Drive and the pier.

The water of the river was a gray color, but it turned to a dirty brown near the shore. Thick with pollution it churned around the ships like hot tar threatening to trap whatever came into its grasp.

The watchmen on duty must have thought I was a cop because he let me be. Someone had left a jar full of fish bait at the end of the pier, and I grabbed it and emptied the contents. Being careful not to fall into the filthy water, I scooped up some of the liquid, put the lid back on, and headed back to the station.

Duke was in his office, and he looked fit to be tied. "Suffocation by drowning."

"Did he check the water in her lungs?"

"I assume he did. Why?"

I handed Duke the jar. "That's water from were Adaline supposedly drowned. What do you think the odds are that it matches what's in her lungs?"

Duke grinned. "Wait here." He was out the door in a flash. When he returned he was smiling from ear to ear. "The assistant to the coroner is being reprimanded for being lazy. And you were right. Clean soapy water was in Adaline Marsh's lungs. The case is back on my desk."

I let Duke get back to his job, and I got on with mine. By the time I got to my apartment, it was pouring down rain, and I was drenched. Cold fingers don't make the most dexterous of hands, and I dropped my keys. In doing so, I noticed that my apartment door had been jimmied. I pulled out my gun and entered. The place was a mess. Cushions ripped, drawers pulled out and emptied, you name it.

When I called the doorman downstairs, he said that no one had come asking for me or was hanging around. He wasn't too happy about hearing my place had been tossed.

With that done, I went in search of Lilian's bag. It was in the bedroom where I left it, but the contents were dumped and the pictures gone. I stepped back and surveyed the damage. Whoever was here wasn't just searching for pictures, they were looking for something small. The inkwell on my desk was dumped along with the salt and pepper shakers in the kitchen.

I looked at my hand and the ring still stuck on my pinky. "You're important to somebody, but why?"

The phone ringing pulled me out of my thoughts. It was Duke.

"I've got dogs asking if Adaline was ever depressed. If she was, it might explain the note. Someone could have picked it up and saved it. As for your curiosity on if Lilian Seadrift ever had a kit, a Chicago hospital has the records. Four years ago, Lilian was an unwed mother and refused to say who the father was. She was listed as a charity case."

"Where's the kit?"

"Stillborn. Crossbreed."

"What about Press?"

"We're picking him up now."

"Good. By the way, my place got tossed. I think they were after the ring."

"Maybe you'd better let me have it for safekeeping."

"Not until Lilian is listed as murder."

CHAPTER 9

Marlow Press had two listings in the directory. The first was the Malibu Club. The second was in Brooklyn's fancy residential district. When I tried the residence, the butler answered and said Press wasn't available and would I like to leave a message. I didn't.

Next, I called Sasha. She recognized my voice right away.

"Hello, darling."

"Hello yourself."

"Am I going to see you again?"

"Hopefully soon. Right now, I got to hunt down a few things, and I need your help. Did you ever know an otter named Adaline Marsh?"

Sasha's voice changed from sultry to worried. "Yes. For several years, in fact."

"I'm sorry to tell you this, sweetheart, but Adaline is dead. Murdered."

"No. Why? How? She was one of us. Adaline was always trying to help those who couldn't..." A soft sob came over the line.

"When I find out, I'll let you know. What I need to know is where his private hangout is. The place he deals with contacts or has private parties."

"He never kept the same one for very long, though he did like the Village."

"Can you give me the address of the last one you remember?"

She did, and I wrote it down.

"You'll have to ask around. Perhaps I could—"

"Nonsense. I know you want to stay as far from this mess as possible, and I don't want to see you hurt. Let me do the searching."

"Be careful. I don't want you to get hurt."

"I'll call you when I'm done to let you know I'm okay."

"Promise?"

"Promise."

It was nice to know someone cared about me. The thought made me feel warm and felt nice, real nice.

After changing into a dry suit, settling my gun in place and donning my trench coat, I was ready to go. The rain outside had gotten worse. Driving was a pain, but I got to the Village and found a parking spot near the address Sasha had given me.

There was a bar not too far away, and I figured it was a good place to start. I ran the distance but still managed to soak my shoes and pant legs. Most of the patrons looked up when I walked in the door, but a pair of male lions only had eyes for each other. A pair of female albatross lost interest quickly as well. A few others had me wondering if I was going to get hit on and wondered how best to turn them down.

The bull behind the bar gave me a knowing smile as I ordered a beer.

"Do you know a guy named Marlow Press? I was supposed to meet him, but I forgot the address." I pulled a twenty out of my wallet and tapped it on the bar.

The bull glanced around. "Press moved to a place over a grocery store about two blocks south down the street."

I paid for my beer, and the bull kept his change. After

finishing my drink, I headed back out into the rain and drove my car down the street to find the store. I parked the car again and did my best not to bolt for cover from the rain. I needed to pay attention to my surroundings.

The mail boxes next to the door for the apartments were both marked. One had the grocer's name. The other for the top floor just said Jones. The first flight of stairs creaked no matter how hard I tried to stay to the edges, but the second had newer boards and were quiet.

My ears picked up noise from inside the apartment, so I pulled out my .45 to be ready for anything. Careful not to make any noise, I eased the door open. Inside the dark apartment, something crashed to the floor.

Someone said, "Keep it down, will yah?"

Easing into the apartment, a shadow came my way, and I could just make out the elk who stumbled in the darkness. Not being able to see, his hand brushed the wall searching for a switch. He got the butt end of my gun instead and was knocked out on the floor.

The place was silent until the other one called out. "You okay, Buck?"

"Yeah," I said.

"Come on back here."

I left my trench coat at the door and moved slowly to the back. Apparently, the elk's name wasn't Buck because I spotted male number two before he could put a bullet in my gut. His gun went off as I rolled for cover and returned fire. Luckily, the second male didn't want to stick around and pulled his groggy companion to his feet but not before blasting a few more holes in the wall.

From the way they both tumbled down the stairs, I figured I'd managed to clip one of them. The thought of giving chase flitted through my head until I heard the screeching of tires outside.

Something valuable was hidden in the apartment, and I meant to find it. Unlike the elk and his friend, I wasn't about to do anything in the dark and hit the light switch.

I put my gun away and looked at the bookcase the elk had been searching. Halfway through my own search, I found the jackpot. A small book stuck in a hollowed-out section of another. I stuffed the book under my belt in the small of my back and decided it was time to leave.

The shouts from outside were getting a little too much, and I didn't want to deal with anyone. I grabbed my trench coat and hat and bolted down the stairs. The open front door stood like a beacon before me, but before I reached it, I was seeing stars, and thunder was roaring in my ears. With the pain which racked my chest came the realization that someone shot me. Everything went blank.

How long I lay there, I don't know. The sound of police sirens had me moving, staggering in the rain toward my car. Pain streaked through my chest with every breath. I crawled inside and must have passed out again because this time when I awoke, the police were gone and there was no sign of a crowd.

The rain still poured down, but all the windows in the buildings were dark.

I felt inside my coat along my chest. Everything still hurt. I hadn't smelt any blood, but when I pulled out my gun, I found out why. The bullet meant for me had destroyed my gun. The slug had hit the top of the slide mechanism, tore it loose, and was now embedded into the blued metal.

"Poor thing. Don't worry. I'll kill the bastard who did this to you. They think they got me, but they didn't."

While lamenting my gun, I checked my back. The book was still there, so I thought of tossing it into the glove compartment. Instead, I shoved it in my coat pocket. Once I felt able to drive, I noticed what was wrong. The ring was gone from my finger.

Things were looking up.

CHAPTER 10

There was a light in the window of Sasha's apartment when I got to her place. I parked the car down a side street and staggered back to her building. The stairs were murder, and I kept having to stop every couple of steps to catch my breath.

I must not have looked so hot when I got to the door because the expression on Sasha's face when she answered my knock was not a joyous one.

"Kaiser? What…? Come in before you fall down."

I did as I was told, but instead of sitting down, I watched every move she made. The green dress she wore looked like it was painted on. When she drew near, I grabbed her by the waist and pulled her close. When I was done nuzzling her neck, I found her lips and gave them the same treatment.

Sasha pulled away and looked up at me. "I think I've fallen in love with you." Before I could say anything, she put her fingers over my mouth. "Don't say anything. Please understand, I need… I want a clean slate."

"You know I don't care about your past."

"But I do. Please, Kaiser?"

I nodded, and she pulled me toward the couch. "Now

tell me what happened."

"Someone shot me, but my gun blocked the bullet. I think they tossed a brick at my head first."

"Lucky for you, you've got a hard head. Did you get them? Who were they?"

"They got away. Don't know who they were either, but they think I'm dead. Plus, they took Lilian's ring."

"Is this a good thing?"

"Possibly." I pulled the book I've found at the apartment out of my coat. "I found what Press' goons were looking for."

Sasha plucked the book from my hands and flipped through the pages. "What is this, some sort of code?"

"Looks it. Take another look through the pages and see if you recognize anything."

This time when she looked through the book, Sasha examined each page. Near the end her ears pitched forward. "This one. I saw him write this symbol one time when he was talking to a client." Her ears flattened to her head, and she bared her teeth. "I ended up with an appointment that night. Some pig from out of town. The male was disgusting."

Without a word, I pulled her close until her fur stopped standing on end. Only then did I call Duke.

"We opened a can of worms, Kaiser."

"You don't say?"

"When we picked up Press, he lawyered up pretty fast, and we couldn't hold him. Didn't even flinch when we told him about Adaline's death. Of course, we let him think she suicided. Press said she was a pain in the rear as an employee, and he was thinking of replacing her. After he left the building is when the avalanche started. The politics in this town must be filthier than I thought."

"Have you found out anything new?"

"Adaline's tub was clean, too clean. Someone did a stellar job of mopping up. The dogs I sent to the Malibu Club got a call from somebody who threatened them, but pit bulls don't scare. They traced the call to a public phone box, but after that lost the trail."

"Well, I've got something new for you. Can you come over here for it?" I gave Duke Sasha's address.

After I hung up the phone, Sasha handed me a beer and pulled me over to her upholstered box in the corner. We both snuggled down in it like a couple of college students looking for cuddles.

When Duke knocked on the door, we untangled ourselves and let him in.

After the introductions he asked, "Where is it?"

I handed over the book and watched him go from wagging tail to droopy everything. "Damn, it's a memory code."

"Can't you break it?"

"Not sure. Each symbol has a meaning known only to the writer. Something like this takes a good memory."

"That book is Press' account book. Sasha recognized one of the symbols."

The news perked Duke up. "Where did you get it?"

"Press has a place down in the Village. Don't ask me to identify the elks I tussled with. It was dark. But they're some of Press' gang. He must have sent them to collect the book."

Duke put the book in his pocket. "I'll call you later once I find out more stuff."

"Let me call you. I'm supposed to be dead."

"What?" Duke's ears flipped forward, and he looked at me intently.

"There was a third person waiting outside. I'm certain it's the same guy who killed Lillian and roughed me up the first time. He thinks I'm dead, and I'd like to let him keep thinking that for a while."

Duke touched the pocket which held the book. "Two different groups of players?"

"That's what I'm thinking. They'll be waiting for my carcass to turn up. Might even think you dogs are keeping my death quiet."

Duke snickered and said his goodbyes.

When he was gone, Sasha piped in and said, "It's going to be an interesting wake."

She handed me a beer. "Tell me about your place getting searched. If they find my place, I want to know what to expect."

I gave her the details, and Sasha grew thoughtful. "He left the baby clothes and took the pictures? I wonder if he looked at the pictures first or just grabbed them."

Curious, I asked, "How do you mean?"

"Remember I told you Lilian had a camera? She used to work for a snapshot place. What if it was a particular set of pictures he was after?"

"That puts us back to James Freely and blackmail. The problem is Caron-Grant alibies Freely for Lilian's murder."

"Couldn't he have slipped out or had someone else kill her?"

"Possible." My mind was racing with thoughts crashing into each other. "Lilian had a camera."

"Yes. She used it for work."

"We, or rather, you have to find that camera. I'm supposed to be dead."

"How?"

"A lot of leg work. We'll need to check every pawn shop in the city."

"That is a lot of leg work." Sasha shifted in her seat so that her dress rode up her thigh.

I reached over and tugged it down. "Yes, it is."

Sasha laughed, got up from the couch, and gave me a kiss. "We should both get some sleep."

CHAPTER 11

The sound of bacon frying awoke me. I got dressed and followed my nose to the kitchen.

"Good morning, sleepy head." Sasha pointed to the table where everything was already set. "You're just in time."

I poured the coffee, and we both settled down for breakfast.

"I called my boss and told him I was feeling under the weather."

"Did he give you any hassle?"

"None. In fact, he seemed concerned."

"Should I be worried about competition?"

Sasha smiled at me. "Maybe. He's an aging mongoose, but a sweet old thing."

She smiled and took a sip of her coffee. "I'll wear something that makes me look like I'm low on money."

"They'll never believe it, you're too gorgeous."

"Oh stop." Sasha reached over and swatted my nose. "Now tell me what I need to do. I don't want to mess this up."

"We'll rip the list out of the classified section of the phone book, basically. When you talk to the males at the counter, don't be anxious. Remember, we're after the address on the pawn ticket more than the camera. You got enough money for a taxi, food, and the camera if you find it?"

"Yes."

I grabbed a piece of paper and pen off the counter. "If you need anything, this is my office and home numbers. This is Duke's in case you can't get me at either place."

"You're not staying here?"

"Not sure yet."

Sasha changed and headed out the door. I called my office.

Instead of giving her usual spiel, Velvet said, "Mr. Wrench is not available at the moment."

"He isn't, is he?"

"No, If you want… Kaiser? Is that you?"

"Have I gotten any calls?"

"Have you… Kaiser, what is going on? The phone has been ringing all morning. Everyone's looking for you, but no one wants to leave a message."

"Who's called?"

"Two Jones, a Smith, and a Wesson."

"A bunch of smart alecks."

"I thought so too. Now would you please tell me what's happened? The only person willing to leave a message was a weasel named Jordy Devonshire."

"Jordy? What did Jordy want?"

"He wouldn't say, but I swear he's been calling all morning."

"Anyone else?"

"Just Caron-Grant. He wanted to know if the check he wrote to the bank went through in time."

I growled. The check was redundant now.

"Listen, Velvet, whatever you do, don't let on that you've heard from me. The only two people you can talk to who know I'm still alive is Duke, and a female named Sasha."

"Still alive? Am I going to get the details, or are you going to leave me hanging?"

"Someone shot at me, but I'm fine. Are you going to write down Sasha's particulars?"

Velvet hissed but wrote down the information. After hanging up, I decided to get my gun replaced. I took a taxi to the other side of town and had them drop me off at a gunsmith. The bear had a few army surplus .45s, and he let me take my pick. With his book signed and money paid, the bear reminded me to call the police and inform them of the new serial number.

I needed to find Jordy next. I tried calling the bars, and his local hangouts, but no dice. No one had seen him. There was only one other option. I took a taxi back to his neck of the woods and looked for a beat cop.

People don't realize how smart cops are, or how much information they acquire. Even if it's just the local gossip.

When I spotted a bloodhound in blue, I followed him for a while. When he stopped in at the local diner for lunch, I took the seat next to him. I had to wait for the bunny sitting next to me to leave before slipping out my badge and license. Sliding them closer to the cop, I kept my voice low. "Keep your nose forward. The name's Kaiser Wrench. Duke Barrow can vouch for me. I need to find Jordy Devonshire."

I could barely see the cop's eyes underneath the wrinkles of skin which covered his face. The bloodhound got up from his seat to use the payphone and was sitting back down within a few minutes. On his way back he grabbed a newspaper someone left at one of the booths.

When he sat back down, he placed the newspaper in front of him and picked up the remains of his sandwich. The hound also took a good size sniff, probably filing the memory of my scent somewhere in the back of his brain.

"You check out," he said softly.

"Good to know. What about Jordy?"

"Scared. He's at a rooming house one block east.

Brownstone with a yellow door."

"Thanks.

I finished my own meal and left the joint heading east. The yellow door was easy to spot. Jordy's little weasel face peered out from behind a curtain on the second floor.

Jordy nearly dragged me into his room when I walked through the door. The weasel was scared.

Once in the room, he babbled. "Kaiser, you gotta help me. How'd you find me? Were you followed? I'm so dead. They're going to nail my pelt to the lamp post as a warning to others. I never should've talked to you. Kaiser, I don't want to die."

"Stop, Jordy. No one is going to find you. Not the way I did. Now, what is it you needed to see me about?"

"They're gonna kill me. I gotta get out of town."

"Who are they?" Before Jordy could start babbling again. I picked him up by the scruff and held him in front of me so that he couldn't look away. "Calm down and tell me, who… are… they?"

Jordy squeaked, "I don't know. Somebody big, real big. Something's going down, and it's huge, Kaiser. Huge. I don't wanna die, Kaiser. These guys… You don't mess with these guys. They know I talked to you."

"How do they know what you said?"

"Does it matter? I'm one dead weasel, Kaiser. You gotta help me."

I set Jordy back down on his feet but didn't remove my hand. Jordy didn't bother to wiggle out from under it either.

"How do you know someone's after you?"

"I spotted them before they spotted me. Big guys. Guys you bring in just for one type of job. I think they were from Detroit. One was this giant moose. You should have seen his rack. It was massive."

"Anybody but me know you're here?"

"Just the mole who runs this place, and she don't care."

Jordy's eyes were as big as saucers as he peered up at

me. "You got an idea?"

"Maybe. Stay here and don't leave this room. Tomorrow at nine-thirty you need to stay calm and walk down the street. Turn right, one block down and head west. Act like you don't have a care in the world."

Jordy stared at me for a second before bursting into tears. "I'm gonna die."

"You're not going to die."

The weasel wiped his eyes and sniffed. "Promise?"

"I promise. But after you do what I say tomorrow, remember one thing."

"Yeah?"

"Yeah. Leave the city and don't come back."

I left Jordy in his room, crying like a kitten and headed north to the subway. When I got there, the train hadn't arrived, so I took the time to check in with both Sasha and Velvet. There was no answer at Sasha's, but Velvet said it'd been a quiet afternoon.

The train took me over to Fifty-Ninth, and I grabbed a cab to where I parked my car. I didn't want to be spotted over near Sasha's place, and keeping an eye out for people who might recognize me was a pain. The rain started again and didn't want to stop. I pulled over near a candy store to sit and think.

One bright idea later, I was inside asking for a directory. I searched the pages for Photo Fast or similar names but found nothing. "Do you have an older book?"

The clerk looked at me through horned rim glasses and legged it to the back. A few minutes later, the stork came back with a dust covered directory that had seen better days. "Here you go. Usually the phone company takes them back, but for some reason they missed this one."

This directory listed Photo Fast on Seventh Ave. The stork let me use the store's phone, but when I tried the number, the operator said it was disconnected. On the way out the door, I spotted the late evening newspapers. Everyone had a headline saying the cops were doing a city wide clean up on vice.

Someone had leaked the news. Duke was going to be furious.

I drove to the address where Photo Fast was located. The office building was old, and the super who answered the door was a bespectacled English badger. I thought he was going to ask me in for tea when he smiled up at me. "Yes?"

"You the super? I'm a private cop that needs to see where Photo Fast used to have its offices."

"Right this way."

The badger showed me to the freight elevator and took me up to the fourth floor. "They were a nice bunch. Good tenants. I'm not really sure why, but the owner closed up shop and left in a hurry. Didn't even tell his employees."

"No one's rented the space since?"

"Oh my, no. There aren't too many people who want to rent an office in this building. Bad neighborhood you see."

He pointed to the door at the far end of the hall. "Room 209."

The door wasn't locked, and I switched on the light. We entered into a room with photos and papers strewn across the floor. The filing cabinets were open and desk drawers removed.

"The room wasn't like this when they left. They were an orderly bunch."

"Someone already searched the place. Did anyone else ask you to see this office?"

"No."

No longer hoping to find anything, I checked a few of the desks and found a box with the name L. Seadrift on the front. At least I had the right place. "Damn."

"I take it you haven't found what you were looking for."

"I'm afraid whoever searched here first may have taken it."

The badger smiled at me again. "Why don't you check the boxes downstairs."

"Downstairs?"

"Yes. One of the employees asked to keep a few things downstairs, but she never came back for them."

My jaw nearly dropped to the floor. Most badgers I've met would sooner roll you for your dough and drop your carcass in the river, after they've stabbed you just for fun that is. This badger was overly helpful.

When I got my mouth working again, I asked, "Was her name Lilian Seadrift?"

"Yes. A very nice vixen."

"I hate to tell you this, but she's dead."

"Oh, dear. How awful."

"Do you mind if I take the stuff she was saving?"

He nodded sadly and took me down to the basement. An accumulation of boxes, junk, receipts, paper, and other items filled the space. Using a flashlight, the badger guided me through the dusty maze to a shelf packed with boxes. Once he found the one he was looking for, he handed it to me.

Inside the box, protected with tissue paper, were more photos. Couples in the park or on the street. A bunch of smiling faces. Each photo bore the date it was taken. Just a bunch of tourist photos.

I thanked the badger and took the box. I'd hoped for an answer, and it seemed I'd reached another dead end.

Duke was at his office when I called but didn't want to talk on the phone. "Can you meet me at Sandy's Grill in fifteen minutes?"

"I'll be there in ten."

When I got to the grill, Duke was sitting in the back booth with a newspaper in front of him. "Did you tell the newspapers what we were up to?"

"You know me better than that. What gives?"

"I'm getting barked at by everyone. Every squirrel and chipmunk that controls a block of votes in this town is in an uproar. Luckily, the D.A. is a hawk above reproach. He knows Adaline Marsh's death is murder, and he's prepared to stick to his guns."

Duke leaned closer, but his eyes scanned our surroundings. "Word got out about the book. But not about the code."

I couldn't help smiling. "And Press' clients are panicking."

"If I continue, I'm looking at forced retirement. If I back down, I might get to keep my job."

"What are you going to do?"

"Not sure."

"You know I got your back."

Duke nodded, but I wasn't about to let go.

"Keep plugging away. There are more books, more records. Somebody will start talking and soon. We keep looking, and the creeps pulling everyone's strings are going to pull too tight. Muscle from out of town has already been hired for jobs."

"How do you know?"

"A weasel told me. We have a trap set up for tomorrow. All I need is your guys to be there, and we can catch and hold a lot of canaries." I told Duke about Jordy Devonshire and what I was up to.

"And he'll go along with the plan?"

"He will. Jordy's scared and has only one way out."

Duke nodded then dropped a bomb. "Marlow Press is missing. No one's heard of him since he left the police station. Also, we searched his home and found some of those same marks from the book. Looks like we'll be able to break that code after all."

CHAPTER 12

The rain didn't want to let up as I made my way to the car. The news of Marlow Press' disappearance didn't disturb me. That beaver was smart and careful. Press would have some sort of insurance against those higher up in the organization. The beaver wasn't dead, just hiding. A lot of other lowlifes would be in hiding or leave the city altogether when this was over.

I parked the car a block away from Sasha's and grabbed the box off the seat next to me. On the walk to her place, I stopped in at a grocery store and picked up cold cuts and a few other things. The bag helped hide my face until I got to her apartment.

Sasha was on the couch with her shoes off and her feet up.

"Honey, I'm home."

"You mean that wasn't a stampede coming up the stairs?" Sasha smiled at me and offered me the towel she'd used to dry her fur off with when she came home. I set the bag and the box on the coffee table and knelt next to the couch. The towel was damp. Her wonderful scent still clung to the material. "How did it go today?"

"Horrid." Sasha sat up and put her arms around my

neck. "I'm cold, wet, hungry, and my feet ache."

After a hello kiss, I said, "The bag has the hungry part set. No cooking either. As for your feet, how about a massage?"

"Sounds divine."

I gave her a good rubdown that had her purring. Before the massage could turn into a tussling match, I grabbed the bag off the coffee table and dropped it into her lap.

"What the?"

"Now for dinner." I picked Sasha up from the couch and carried her to the kitchen.

"But what about my massage? I was enjoying that."

"You also said you were hungry."

Sasha gave me a devilish grin as I set her in a chair. "I also said I was cold and wet. Is an old fashion tongue bath somewhere in the picture?"

"Behave."

I put the coffee on while Sasha divvied up what was in the bag and used the wrappings as plates.

"So, tell me how you fared with the pawn shops."

Sasha bit into one of the meat slices instead of putting it on her sandwich. "Elimination only I'm afraid. None of the fifteen shops I visited had the camera. When you consider how many shops are in the city, it'll take forever."

"Unfortunately, it's the only lead we've got."

"Someone else is looking for that camera."

Her words sent the fur on my back straight up. "Who?"

"A hyena. One clerk mentioned he was looking for a commercial camera but didn't look at any. Just asked about one and left."

"That's a coincidence I don't like."

"Kaiser, I'm not afraid."

"What if it's not a coincidence and he finds out you're looking for the same camera? You could get hurt."

"If you hadn't noticed, I'm a big snow leopard. I know

how to take care of myself. And a good knee to the groin can bring even the largest ox to the ground. Screaming is also a good way of scaring off an insistent male."

I opened my mouth to object, but she interrupted.

"Stop worrying. I'll be careful. Now tell me how your day went."

"I found the place Lilian used to work. Someone got there before me, but since they didn't talk to the building supervisor, they didn't get the box she had stashed in the basement."

"Anything interesting?" Sasha's ears came forward, and she quickly cleaned up the mess in front of her. "Let's see. Do you have them?"

I got up and went to grab the photos out of the box I left on the coffee table. "It's just work pictures, but I guess she stuck them in the basement for some reason."

Separating the pile into two stacks I handed one to Sasha. The first few photos I scoured for anything that was unusual, but it soon became apparent they all followed the same tourist pattern. In two of the shots, the male tried to hide his face. I set both aside when what little I could see, I thought I recognized.

Sasha gasped. "It's Tina."

"Who?"

"One of the females that…" Sasha looked away. "We sometimes went on dates together." She handed me the photo. A smiling doe stood next to a not so happy looking deer.

"Do you recognize the stag?"

"No."

I put the picture next to the two others I'd set aside. A few minutes later, Sasha spotted another female she knew. The pair of dogs were as different as night and day. The dame was an elegant Afghan hound, and the male was an overstuffed bulldog dressed in clothes that were designed to make him look taller.

Sasha put the photo next to the others we'd set aside.

"She married one of the clients and got out as soon as she could."

On a hunch, I reached over and checked the back of the card. Written in Lilian's elegant script was a reference letter and number. Where had Lilian stashed the reference file?

The next big find came from my stack. The people in the forefront weren't important, but in the background was James Freely. The hyena was holding the car door for Caron-Grant. Also on the street was Roman Chase. The Alpine ibex's face was a mask of fear as the hyena sneered in triumph. The old fox, his back to the pair, smiled, oblivious to the scene behind him.

I must have growled because Sasha grasped my arm. "What is it, Kaiser?"

"The goat with the massive horns in this photo is Roman Chase. He's dead. The hyena is James Freely."

"That can't be."

"It is. Freely worked for Caron-Grant until I got him fired."

"But that's Brandon Hubert, one of the males who supply the houses with females."

"What?"

Sasha took the photo from my grasp. "I'm sure it's him. Hubert worked out west somewhere but came east for some reason."

"Well, he had a nice legit job as cover until I blew it for him. Do you recognize the male he's grinning at?"

"Yes. Chase, wasn't it? He was murdered."

I took back the picture and gave it another once over. Caron-Grant looked like he was entering the bar entrance of the Whitefish Club. How close the place was to where Chase was found murdered I didn't know, but I wouldn't have been surprised to find out it wasn't far.

"What's on the back?"

At Sasha's question, a letter and number range was written. "About a dozen pages of information goes with this picture. If only we could figure out where the files are."

"Or what they contain."

We each looked through our stacks again before switching. I didn't find anything else, but Sasha came up with another dozen females she recognized. Each one stood next to a male whose appearance stank of money. On every photograph, a notation was written on the back.

The photos we pulled out of the stack, I put in an envelope and stuck it in the back of a kitchen drawer. The other photos I put back in the box. Too antsy to sit down, I paced the floor, thinking. Freely was up to his eyeballs in the racket but hid under a guise of respectability. Just how was he connected to Lilian? Was it plain blackmail or something else?

"I need a drink."

"You're supposed to be playing dead."

"That doesn't mean we can't go out for a drink. Grab your coat and hat and let's go."

The rain outside poured down, so we found a taxi, and it took us to a bar. On the way, we passed the now closed Malibu Club. Neither of us wanted to go to a crowded place, so we had the cabbie drop us off at a corner dive.

We took a seat at the bar and ordered our drinks. The profession was as old as life itself, but others besides the females were making money. Freely, Roman, Marlow, even Jordy all got their cut. The thought of the extra five hundred I'd given Adaline Marsh flitted through my head, and I realized I needed to return the cash. The otter would not have had time to cash the check I gave her.

"I need to pay a bill."

After we paid our tab, Sasha followed me to the Whitefish Club. "Are you going to tell me what's going on in that head of yours?"

"If I could, I would. Some of the puzzle pieces fit, but not everything."

Unlike the dingy bar we left or the glitz of the Malibu

Club, the Whitefish Club was all dark mahogany and thick rich carpets. We never got past the anteroom. Sasha spotted Freely before I did and grabbed my arm. The hyena was standing at the bar drinking and smiling like there was no tomorrow. Next to him, stood the African wild dog from the carpark.

"What are we going to do? You're not going after him, are you?"

"No." As much as I wanted to gut Freely, I knew this wasn't the time. There was no evidence of Freely ever having done something wrong. Not to mention, I was supposed to be playing dead.

I hustled our butts out of the place and back onto the street before either Freely or his buddy spotted us. Two blocks down the street and around the corner, I found a phone booth and called Duke at his home.

"It's Kaiser. I just spotted Freely at the Whitefish Club with a wild dog that I had an argument with a few days ago. Would you mind putting a tail on him for me?"

"I'll do better than that. I'll arrest him. A teletype came in from the west coast. The hyena's wanted for murder."

"Murder? Who did he kill and why?"

"A pelican by the name of Percy Smith. Not sure what started the bar brawl, but Freely started with a knife and ended up using his fists. He broke the pelican's neck."

A chilling tingle ran up my spine at the news, and I rubbed the spot under my ear where the flesh had been sore. Anger followed when I realized who kept stealing the ring.

"Race you to the bastard."

I hung up the phone and bolted from the box. Sasha chased after me, but I wasn't about to stop. I wanted to pummel Freely into the pavement. Police sirens filled the air, urging me to get there first. Up ahead, I could see the yellow light of a cab along with another car as it pulled away from the Whitefish Club. By the time I got there, Freely and his buddy were gone.

After questioning the bartender, I found out the place had a radio. Freely had paid the bartender to keep it on the police channel.

CHAPTER 13

Sasha caught up to me, and Duke wasn't far behind. Wanting to avoid curious onlookers, we went back outside to talk and let the police dogs handle the crowd.

"Did you see the car Freely got into?" asked Duke.

"Dark with a side of dark. The doorman wasn't much help either. That bird can't tell a Buick from a Bentley."

A reporter tried slipping past the police line, but a Newfoundland caught the squirrel by the tail and tossed him back over the barrier. Not wanting anyone to find out I was still among the living, I kept my back to the crowd. Sasha stayed by my side.

"How's it on your end, Duke?"

"I'm catching hell from all directions. Even the newspapers are wondering what's going on. But I can dish out just as much as I get." Duke gave me a toothy grin. "I had a group of handpicked dogs pull a few raids on some fancy uptown houses. The game they caught would make your eyes pop. Not only do we have names but charges to go with them. Plus, those who tried to bribe their way out of trouble dug their hole deeper."

"They're running scared. And I might be able to contribute more than I originally thought."

"How so?"

"Lilian was doing more than petty blackmail. If I'm right. You might have all the proof you need to break the racket. Are you ready for tomorrow night?"

"Yes, I'm ready." Duke tossed the cigarette he was smoking into the gutter. "Sometimes I wonder if I actually run my department. The dogs are selected, but I haven't told them what they're doing yet. I don't want anyone yapping their head off."

The crowd was thinning out, but the reporters seemed to multiply. Not wanting to be recognized, we left Duke to deal with them. Sasha and I went back to her place to relax.

She turned the radio on low, and we both snuggled up on the couch. I must have dozed off because I awoke to her fingers tracing the scars on my face.

"Your stripes don't line up, and it makes you look ruthless, but there's a kindness in you."

Where her fingers traveled, her lips followed. Sweet and powerful, she was in control. I didn't want her to pull away, but she was in command and slipped into the bedroom. A few minutes later, she called to me, and I followed.

Sasha stood in the room, wearing a gown so close fitting and so white she looked like a marble statue. "This gown was supposed to be for a wedding in another life. That life never happened. I forgot that life until I met you."

She stepped forward and ran her fingers along my chin. "I think... No. I know I love you Kaiser. Could you ever...?"

"I love you."

She smiled up at me. "Then give me a night I can remember."

Her lips were warm and her arms inviting. It would be a night I wouldn't forget.

The next morning, I woke up to an empty bed. Sasha had left a note on the dresser with a lipstick kiss as a signature. She'd gone off to find the camera.

With the realization that I'd slept the entire morning away, I hurried to get dressed. The radio was still on and the announcer was talking fast. Duke's dogs had made at least two other raids and were pulling in shady characters left and right.

The big guys in the racket had pushed Duke, and Duke was biting back. Only this time, the newspapers had picked up on the case and were determined to drive it home. The resulting public outcry was going to make sure Duke and his dogs were going to get a fair run.

I grabbed the phone and called Duke at the office. "How's everything going?"

"Splendid. The rats are talking, but all we can get is the clients and how the racket worked. We still don't have the big guy."

"The clients financed everything. Make them pay."

"Oh, they will all right. And guess what, Marlow Press has been spotted in the city."

"Press is still here? Why?" I scowled, trying to reason out the beaver's motivation.

"Guess he wants to see how things pan out."

"He's in for a surprise."

"Well, here's another surprise. There's a bunch more tough guys in town, but we can't touch them. Not yet anyway. So far, they've kept their noses clean. We're not sure what they're up to, but we're trying to keep an eye out for them."

I let out a growl. "I smell money. The big guy plans on staying in business and is using outside thugs to try to keep others quiet. He's retrenching."

"And doing well at it. Seems his thugs got to the right parties before we could."

"Damn."

"You can say that again."

Picking up the telephone cradle, I paced the floor as far as the cord would let me. "You going to be there tonight?"

"Of course, but if the D.A. finds out I'm working with you, I'll have some serious explaining to do."

"You can handle it. Sasha's still working on her end. If she manages to find what we're looking for, the D.A. won't say boo to you. If she calls you, don't ask any questions. Just do what she says."

"Okay, I will."

I hung up and called long distance to connect me with Caron-Grant's home. When the butler answered, he informed me that Caron-Grant was in the city and staying at the Summit. After I hung up on him, I tried contacting Velvet. She must have been out to lunch because I let the phone ring, but no one picked up.

I put the phone back and grabbed my coat. Curious about the jiggling noise I heard, I investigated my pockets and came up with a spare set of apartment keys for Sasha's place. I couldn't help grinning like an idiot.

The rain was still trying to drown the city, so I ducted into a bar to stay dry. The bartender had the radio on and every few minutes the announcer interrupted with breaking news.

Two hours later, I decided to call the Summit. I put my coin in the telephone and waited for the desk clerk to answer. When he did, he said that Caron-Grant had just arrived, and would I like to leave a message. I didn't, so I thanked him and hung up.

At around six-thirty, I had dinner and drove around town. When I got tired of wasting time, I parked close to Jordy's apartment and settled down to wait.

When nine-thirty finally came around, Jordy exited his place and did as he was told. Even with the rain, he didn't run. Nobody was in sight. Waiting until he turned the corner, I started the car and drove around to the next street. Once I had the car parked, I picked up Jordy's tail and followed on the opposite side of the street.

Both of us got a scare when a car drove slowly past the weasel and stopped. One lush of a bear poured himself out of the vehicle and headed straight for the bar.

Other than a beat cop, Jordy and I were alone on the street. Or so I thought. The guy wanted Jordy's death to be up close and personal. Jordy screamed when the bull came down the apartment steps, gun in hand, but never got off a shot. The dark blue horde came out of the shadows and was on him before he could pull the trigger. Roaring mad, the bull wasn't about to go down without a fight.

Four things happened at once. A gun went off, the sound followed by a second, Jordy screamed and bolted down the street, and the bull's body jerked and fell in slow motion to the pavement. The sound of several other shots echoed down from somewhere up the street. One of the police dogs spotted me, and I identified myself. "Kaiser Wrench, Private Investigator."

"I recognize you."

A prowl car roared around the corner, and soon the street was full of cops and searchlights.

I ignored the pandemonium when another car pulled up next to me and Duke got out.

"Evening," he said.

"Where were you at?"

"Busy tailing the tough guys." Duke grinned at me. The sound of more gunshots and a scream had Duke's ears down and growling. "Damn. We're getting as bad as you.

CHAPTER 14

I climbed into my car and turned on the radio. Every news channel was saying the same thing about the raids and takedowns. The repetition had me turning the thing off on the drive.

Since Caron-Grant was in the city, I decided to try again to hand back the extra cash he'd sent. The old fox wanted to be remembered, and he was going to be when this was all finished.

When I pulled up to the Summit, I handed my keys to the bellboy for him to park the car and went inside. Stepping into the place was like walking into another time. A quiet gentlemens only place that smelled of tobacco and polish. The desk clerk told me Caron-Grant was in his rooms but was reluctant to disturb him. With a little cajoling, I managed to convince the old bird that Caron-Grant knew me and would welcome my dropping by.

There's nothing a clerk likes worse in a quiet building than having a tiger threaten to start roaring and wake up the guests.

Not sure if the old bird was more shaken by my audacity or Caron-Grant's agreement to see me. The clerk gave me the room number, and I bounded up the stairs.

When I entered Caron-Grant's room, I got a surprise. It wasn't just a room but a suite that must have taken up a good section of the fourth floor. No expense was spared in the decoration either.

Caron-Grant smiled and shook my hand. "How nice to see you. Given the time, I take it you come bearing good news?"

"Yes and no. Sometimes I just need someone to talk to, and since I needed to return the extra money you sent me, I figured I'd stop by."

The old fox motioned me into a chair and asked, "Are you referring to the money I sent for the extra expenses?"

"Yes. Like a dope, I didn't consider being tailed. The poor otter didn't get a chance to cash the check."

"Oh, dear. Does that mean?" Caron-Grant looked up at me in bewilderment.

"She was murdered. Her death was made to look like a suicide, but the killer made a mistake. The same party broke into my apartment and searched the place. They took off with some stuff, but nothing that I'd call evidence."

The old fox fidgeted in his chair. "Do you know who it was that…?"

"James Freely, your ex-employee. The hyena is wanted out west for murder. Apparently, he was using his position with you along with a false name as a cover."

"Oh my. That's dreadful." Caron-Grant gripped his hands together, closed his eyes, and let a soft whine escape his lips as his ears flattened to his head. "What have I done?"

"Listen, you didn't do anything. James Freely used you. He would have used anybody."

Caron-Grant opened his eyes and looked at me but said nothing.

"Have you heard what's going on in the city?"

"Are you referring to what the newspapers have been reporting?"

"Yes. Your money got you that. A sense of decency. You hired me to find a name. Instead, I found a dumpster full of scum. There's still a long way to go, but we'll get to the bottom of everything."

"The female, have you found out anything?" Caron-Grant's eyes narrowed.

"Yes, and no. There's still questions that need to be answered. Plus, her family still hasn't been found. Speaking of which, can I use your phone?"

"Of course, it's in the other room. Why don't I mix us some drinks while you make your call? I'm not used to stressful news and could use one."

The sadness in the old fox's eyes wasn't easy to watch, and I kicked myself for not giving the news to him in a more polite way. Then again, how else could I have talked about murder? The newspapers were dishing out the information about all the rest.

Once I found the phone, I called Velvet at home. She wasn't too pleased.

"Now you call me. Do you have any idea how long I waited at the office? That female you told me about sent me a pawn ticket by special messenger. Nothing else, no note, just a pawn ticket."

"Hallelujah. She found it."

"Found what?"

"What did you do with the ticket?"

"Left it at the office."

"Meet me at the office in an hour and thirty."

"But—"

"Don't argue, I don't have my keys on me."

Before Velvet could say another word, I held down the hook to disconnect and dialed Sasha. She answered on the second ring.

"Kaiser?"

"Hi, Honey."

"Kaiser, I found it. Did you get the envelope?"

"I just talked to Velvet. It's at the office. Where did you

find it?"

"In a shop just off the Bowery. There it was, hanging in the window. I kept the camera but was afraid to keep the pawn ticket."

"What happened?"

"Remember that hyena I told you about who was searching for a camera?"

My hand tightened on the handset. "Yes."

"Several clerks said that he came in just before me. So, I switched to the end of my list, and there it was. I was still spooked, so I sent the ticket to your office."

"Smart and gorgeous. I'm a lucky guy. Love you to pieces."

"Please, Kaiser."

"When this is over, we got our whole lives to look forward to. Do you love me?"

"You know I do."

"I'll see you soon. Love you."

When I came back into the other room Caron-Grant handed me the drink he mixed. "Good news?"

"Yes. I believe we've found the answer to all our questions."

"Will there be more… death?" He moved toward a phonograph, opened the lid, and lowered the needle. The sound of an opera filled the room.

"Maybe."

I was halfway through my drink when he asked, "Would you like another? I was thinking of having another, but I don't want to drink alone."

Feeling like a heel, I agreed. The old guy wasn't used to the underside of life, and I dropped it right in his lap. While he was off getting another drink, I made out the check and left it on the table. To keep from being antsy, I lit up a smoke.

When Caron-Grant came back into the room, he not only had a bottle but a bucket of ice.

"Do you mind telling me the reasons for everything

happening? Perhaps I could rest easier if I knew a little more. I don't need all the gory details, just an overview."

"Sure. I was hunting for a name and stumbled over a crime. That crime led me to other names. Big names. The police have taken over the crime aspect, and they're not stopping until they've trailed everything to the end."

Not wanting to get sloshed as I expected the fox might end up doing, I sipped my drink before adding, "You should be proud for having a hand in the cleanup."

"Should I?"

"Lilian might not have made it, but I know of at least one other who got out of the business."

"If only we could have done something for the female. But like you said, if the female had an illegitimate child and let her life spiral down, then who can be blamed? A life of sin only brings darkness." He shook his head. "Too bad these females don't take pride in themselves. What's wrong with them?"

"Double standards for the most part. Everyone makes the same mistakes, it's just a few that get caught in a trap and can't find their way out. If their families turn their back on them, where do they go? What do they do? It's not easy going it alone, and if you have young to support." I shrugged my shoulders and looked away.

We sat in silence, and I lit another cigarette. After a while I checked my watch and decided it was best to leave.

"The check I owe you is on the table. If you don't mind, I should get going. I'll let myself out."

Caron-Grant nodded in agreement.

I slipped out the door and hustled down the stair. With a quick wave to the desk clerk, I was out the door. Once I picked up my car, I was off to the office.

Velvet met me in the lobby about fit to be tied.

"Can't you read a clock?"

"I got distracted."

"You're always distracted. Usually by something with legs." If Velvet had a tail, it would have been swishing all over the place she was so mad.

We signed the night book and the skunk operating the elevator took us up to our floor.

Velvet's ears turned this way and that sending the tufts on the ends flipping all over the place. "Are you going to tell me what's going on?"

"The Arctic fox pawned her camera. That's why the pawn ticket. Blackmail and a lot of it. Duke is going to need the evidence."

She gave me one of her evil lynx glares and stormed off the elevator toward the office. After rummaging in her purse for the keys, she opened the door and flipped on the lights.

I walked past Velvet to her desk. "Where is it?"

"On the desk, right…" Velvet walked up next to me and pointed. With confusion on her face, she looked around her desk and glanced at the floor. "It's gone."

"What?"

Velvet touched a pad of paper on her desk, her eyes wide. "The number and address are gone too."

"Whose?"

"Sasha's."

"No, no, no." I grabbed the office door to check the lock. The telltale scratches were there. The elevator operator was looking at me from the open door of the lift, and I yelled. "Did anyone come up here this evening?"

"No. It's been a real quiet night."

"Could anyone have gotten up here without you noticing?"

"Guess so. Me and the attendant have been busy mopping the floors."

Velvet slipped into the elevator car before me and had the skunk take us back to the lobby. I didn't wait for the skunk to open the doors but did it myself and made a run for my car. With the accelerator floored that car still didn't go as fast as I wanted, and I blew through a couple of lights.

I jumped the curb in front of Sasha's place and would have ripped the door off the hinges if I could. Once inside the building, I bounded up the stair.

The smell of blood hit me before I saw her. Bright red across her snowy fur. Sasha was on the floor with her arms out.

"No." I went to her and dropped to my knees. The wound was still flowing, and her breath was short gasps.

"Sasha."

Her eyes opened at the sound of my voice. My innards twisted when she smiled at me. The look of fear overtook her smile, and as she tried to speak, she looked away from me toward the door. Before she could say a word, she was gone.

Rage consumed me as my own blood thundered in my ears. I almost didn't hear the sound behind me or the shadow of movement, but I recognized the smell. James Freely.

CHAPTER 15

If I hadn't turned when I did, Freely would have buried the knife in my back. Instead, it sliced through my coat.

Had it sliced through my skin, I doubt if I would have noticed. Fury narrowed my vision, and I lashed out with my claws, clipping Freely and opening a line of flesh across his jaw.

Freely had sense enough to run, but he didn't get far. I caught hold of his coat and wasn't about to let go. There wasn't much room on the landing outside the apartment, but he managed to twist around and slash with his blade at my face. Another scar to add to my assortment.

Somehow, he managed to slip out of the coat, but he lost the knife when I knocked it out of his grasp. I could have cared less if any of his punches landed. One misstep and we both tumbled down the stairs. Freely might have gotten away if I hadn't landed on him.

With one clawed hand, I pinned his head to the floor and opened his belly with the other. I didn't stop until pieces covered the landing. After that, I roared myself hoarse in frustration and pain.

The sound of police sirens and shouting seeped into my brain. Some scrap of thought had me searching

Freely's pockets for the cardboard stub of the pawn ticket which had cost Sasha her life. My hand closed around it before the police dogs arrived with guns drawn.

I didn't resist as they pulled me down the stair and out of the building. With my anger spent, I felt numb. One of the officers took my statement.

How much time I spent in the back of the police car until Duke arrived, I don't know. But I went from crazed killer to private detective on a mission. Freely's knife was found along with Sasha's body.

Duke had one of the officers take me home and another one drive my car back to my apartment. He'd wanted me to stay put, but I needed a drink, and I was out of beer.

I wandered down the street to the Shipwreck Bar and banged on the back door. Albert was an albatross with his own private stash. He opened the door in his pajamas ready to chew out whoever had woken him. The argument fled his beak as soon as he saw me. "Come on in, Kaiser."

Albert led me to the bar and poured me a drink. "Do you want to talk about it?"

"He killed her. That mangy hyena killed her, but I got him. Tossed his innards all across the floor." I slugged the drink down and handed the glass out for more. "Did you know the last words I said to her? I told her I loved her, and I did too."

I fumbled in my coat pocket for a cigarette and came up with the pawn ticket. The name Lilian Seadrift stared back at me along with the name of a Coney Island hotel.

"He planned to murder my Arctic fox, but that didn't go quite how he planned. She got hit by a car first. He would have killed me too if Press had let him."

Freely, I knew, had tipped off Press. I couldn't get anywhere in this case without tripping over Freely, and the ring. The ring kept nagging me. Where was it now? Was it a crucial piece of the puzzle?

Gazing at the bottles lining the back of the bar, things

slowly fell into place. The answer had been staring me right in the face the whole time. The three feathers emblem on one of the bottles was similar to the ones on Caron-Grant's tomb. The same as the fleur-de-lis on the ring.

Albert tried stopping me, but I was out the door and heading for my car before he could do anything but screech a protest.

The files were at the hotel. They had to be. Lilian had no money, she would have left everything she owned there, knowing they would be held until she could retrieve them.

The hotel in question was closed for the season. Just to be safe, I parked a block away and walked back. The place wasn't high-end. If anything, it was barely hanging on to business. Not bothering with the front entrance, I hopped the fence next to one of the concession stands and stepped around back.

The rain started again, obscuring any trace in the sand of my passing. The roof of one of the shacks slanted in a way that made it easy for me to climb up. From there, I was able to reach one of the windows and gain entrance to the hotel. The lock on the window didn't quite work, and it gave with a bit of pressure. Once inside, I used my penlight to search.

Garbage cluttered the floor of the room I'd entered and the hallway I stepped into. The aging hotel would have been used as a flophouse at the best of times, but the thought of someone breaking into the place worried me. What if what I was looking for was already gone?

Narrow hallways, worn carpet, and empty rooms were accompanied by the ever-present smell of dry rot. The storage room I was looking for had a nice size padlock on the door. The lock was old, and it didn't take much to tease it open with a set of lock picks I kept stashed in the car.

Everything of value in the hotel was there, stacked all

nice and neat. Glassware, mattresses, sheets, and old luggage. A couple of windows lined one wall and gave me a small amount of light to keep me from tripping over anything. That didn't keep me from dropping my penlight and breaking the thing. I managed to find an old oil lamp on one of the shelves and lit it with a match I kept for my cigarettes.

What I was looking for, turned out to be a small trunk with Lilian's name stenciled on the front. When I got the thing open, the number of files it contained left little room for any additions.

Lilian wasn't a blackmailer, but a whistleblower. Filled with pictures, documents, and notes, the trunk contained everything needed to take down the racket.

A noise caught my attention, so I closed and relocked the case. Before I rose from the floor, I pulled my gun and turned.

I sniffed the air, trying to get a sense of who was there, but the blood which spattered my clothes messed with my nose. The roar of a gun firing along with the bullets slamming into my chest and leg knocked me to the floor. Had Caron-Grant been a better shot, he could have gotten me in the head. The next two shots went wild as the old fox swore a blue streak. One of the shots hit the lantern I'd been using. Flaming oil splattered the shelf where I'd left it and ignited everything around it.

I didn't bother rolling for cover but managed to return fire, hitting Caron-Grant in the hip. He screamed in pain and writhed on the floor. His eyes were mad with hate. He seemed oblivious of the tinderbox we were in or the fast-rising flames.

The fox was insane. He'd distracted me long enough to contact Freely to retrieve the pawn ticket and kill Sasha. Caron-Grant, with all his respectability, had been the puppet master all along.

"Lilian Seadrift was your granddaughter, and you had Freely murder her."

My declaration sent the old fox into a screaming fit and blasting the shelves above my head.

"Was it the fact that she was pregnant out of wedlock that pissed you off or that she was carrying a crossbreed?"

From the string of obscenities that came out of Caron-Grant's mouth, Lilian must have been shocked to find out the family money was gone, replaced by a new income source. Freely's attempt to kill her didn't work quite right. Lilian had managed to get up and stagger away. Had she not been clipped by a car and fallen, she might have survived. Lilian hadn't been drunk when she was hit but reeling from Freely's attack.

The sound of firetrucks coming to the rescue didn't sit well with me. They'd concentrate on us and leave the trunk to burn. Caron-Grant couldn't get away with what he'd done. I wasn't about to let his name go down in history untarnished.

I rolled back over to the trunk and put my weight behind it, sliding it toward the window. Somehow, I managed to lift the trunk and shove it through the window, breaking the glass. The influx of air sent the flames higher and Caron-Grant wailing in anger. He didn't seem to notice that his fur was on fire.

Outside, I could hear the firemen shouting. I turned to Caron-Grant and said, "Lilian will be in that tomb. Not you."

Even wounded, I was a damn good shot, and I planted one right between the old fox's eyes. If I got out of this mess, I'd tell everyone that the body found in the flames was just another lackey. Lucius Caron-Grant was going to disappear, and there wouldn't be enough left of him for the carrion eaters.

OTHER BOOKS BY
STACY BENDER

Ursa Kane
I Like Alice
Man on the Stair
Malum

Boxers & Briefs: Book of Shorts

The Sav'ine Series:
Emerald Tears
Hands of Onyx
Diamond Mind
Sons of Amethyst
Moonstone Child
Bloodstone Reborn
Pearl of Sorrow

(Written under Catherine Bender)

Dead Letter
Body in the Boot

BOOKS BY
STACY BENDER & REID MINNICH

Bad Sushi & Other Tails

The Kawokee Series:
Kawokee
The Right to Belong
Heretic

COLLECT ALL THIRTEEN POACHED PARODIES OF KAISER WRENCH

I, the Tribunal
My Claws are Quick
Retribution is Mine!
A Solitary Evening
The Great Slay
Pet Me Fatal
The Female Trackers
The Worm
The Contorted Figure
The Figure Fans
Existence…Eliminated
The Carnage Male
Dark Lane

ABOUT THE AUTHOR

P.C. Hatter is the fursona of Stacy Bender. A mix of Mad Hatter and the Cheshire Cat, Purple Cat Hatter can be seen at most conventions she attends.
The author lives in Cincinnati with her husband and cat.

She loves to hear from readers. Contact her at
stacycbender@gmail.com

Sign up for news
Members are the first to know about upcoming releases, events and deals.
www.stacybender.net

Made in the USA
Columbia, SC
23 June 2024

37405212R00062